Secrets on the Breeze

Hazel McIntyre

Hazel McIntyre

Moran Communications

First Published in Ireland by
Moran Communications
December 2001

ISBN 0 9524426 2 0

Typset: Stuart Clarke
Proof Reading: Denise Cavanagh
Cover Design: Ivan Johnston

Printed and bound in Ireland by:
Browne Printing, Letterkenny, Co Donegal

I would like to thank my family and friends for their support and encouragement particularly my husband Charles, Stuart, Robert, Colleen, wee Darragh, Denise Cavanagh, Michelle Mc Cole, Dessie Kearney and all my goods friends in Inishowen and Derry.

About the Author

Internationally renowned Hazel McIntyre, is the author of five books of memoir and fiction that bring the past alive with a unique storytelling style that stuns and holds the reader to the very end.
Hazel was born on a farm in the Innishowen peninsula of Co. Donegal in Ireland.
After leaving school she moved to London where she became a nurse, before marrying husband Charles.
They later moved back to Ireland, in the 1970s and have three grown up children.

Her first book 'Iron Wheels on Rocky Lanes' which vividly recalled her Donegal childhood was first published in 1994 to an outstanding ovation from the critics. Her first work of fiction 'For Love of Mary Kate' was published in 1996 and told the powerful and compelling tale of three generations of women in 1920s rural Ireland. It was hailed by newspaper critics as 'the first of many fine novels from this emerging Donegal writer.' 'For Love of Mary Kate' was chosen by Woman's Way magazine as their choice for their Millennium edition as 'the most compelling read'.

Hazel McIntyre's novel 'Lament In The Wind' was launched in October 1999. Beginning in the present, the carefully researched work of fiction set against the background of famine Ireland, tells the compelling story of Cassie O' Connor.

'Lament in the wind' is not only Hazel McIntyre's tribute to the victims of The Great Hunger, but is also a tribute to the courage and dignity of the human spirit.

In addition to her role as writer, housewife and mother Hazel McIntyre runs creative writing classes, gives talks to women's groups and support groups throughout Ireland. Her unique and witty observations have captivated radio and television audiences in Ireland, the UK, the USA and Canada.

Hazel's books have been used by both second and third level students in Ireland who have used her writings as a supplement to course work,

Whispering
Whispering voices among the reeds
Is this a love in darkness wrought?
Longer than memory, a thought
Deeper than the grave of time
My root of the world from which all
New springs shall grow....

Chapter 1

Dublin

Mary Kate Quinn looked fondly down at her class of seven and eight year-olds. As far back as she could remember, teaching was all she ever wanted to do and she had never once regretted that calling.

The school was situated in the midst of a run down, inner city area that filled the lives of its inhabitants with grinding poverty. Mary Kate marvelled at the cheerful, dignified way in which they accepted their lot.

Glancing at the clock, she said, "Put your books away. It's time for the next chapter of *The Secret Garden*". The sheer pleasure on their small faces tugged at her heartstrings. She wanted more than anything to bring a little joy into their drab young lives. And as far as the children were concerned, Miss Quinn was the brightest, most beautiful thing in their world.

When she had finished the chapter, a chorus of voices from the desks below asked, "Please Miss, read a bit more. Two chapters." Amidst the chorus of disappointment, she heard a loud urgent knock on the classroom door. The head teacher, Mary Reardon stood in the doorway when she opened it.

"I want to talk to you. Outside," she said. From the narrow set of her eyes Mary Kate knew that she was in for another humiliating lecture. "Miss Quinn," she began. "You are here to teach the children; discipline is the first priority for a good teacher. Spare the rod and spoil the child, is a very true saying. And from the racket coming from that classroom of yours you have not learned that important principle." She glared at her young colleague with a look of spiteful contempt. She resented her youth, her good looks, the way the male teachers looked at her, and spoke about her.

They stared at each other for a moment in mutual contempt. Then Mary Kate said quietly, "I was reading them a chapter from a book. They were just asking me to read a little more. You see I believe it's important to encourage them to read; to learn about the joys of literature at the earliest possible age."

"*Joys ... joys.* Who do you think you are? You are

here to teach them what they need to know to survive in the world. Joy doesn't come into it." The spiteful, angry look on her face made Mary Kate shudder.

"I will see to it that you get shifted away from this school as soon as possible," she said, shooting another contemptuous look at Mary Kate, before storming off back into the school. A deep flush spread across Mary Kate's cheeks; she felt that she was being sent packing like a servant.

Back in the classroom Mary Kate dismissed her class and stood at the window watching them go out the gate. The four children from the orphanage walked away together in a huddled group. They were always dressed in the same clothes and had that air of sadness about them. Mary Kate tried to give them that little bit of extra attention; to praise their efforts, and maybe give them hope for a happier future. As she watched their backs disappear around the corner, she thought again about her own beginnings in an orphanage. Had she not had the love and courage of her grandmother, she too might have been in the same boat. She sighed deeply at the memory of the encounter with Mary Reardon. She was baffled by her spiteful hostility towards her, and had tried to explain her teaching methods to her, and how well her class was progressing. But she simply wouldn't listen. "I don't want any explanations from a slip of a girl like you, when I have been teaching all my life," she had said, cutting off any further discussion. Suddenly Mary

Secrets on the Breeze

Kate felt a painful, pang of homesickness. She could picture her grandmother and her father sitting at either side of the drawing-room fire; she remembered the happy times they had spent in that room, talking by the sighing embers late at night.

And she was again overcome with a longing to talk to them, and feel the comfort of their love. She always thought of James Thompson as her father, even though she knew that he was not her biological one. Sometimes late into the night when she couldn't sleep, she would wonder who her father really was. It was comforting to make believe that James Thompson really was her father, and for some credible reason had to keep it a secret.

Mention of her father in her grandmother's hearing would bring a look of anxiety bordering on fear and so she had learned to ponder in silence. 'Why do I want to know about who my father was? Why does it matter so much?' she asked herself again, as she had so often done in the past. She couldn't quite explain, even to herself, why she needed to know so desperately. Was it the secrecy that surrounded her very existence?

Her attention was drawn away from thoughts of home by the sudden appearance of her colleague John Flynn. He was a broad shouldered man in early middle - age with a shock of dark hair falling across his forehead. He knocked quietly on the classroom door and opened it before she had time to answer. Walking over to a desk close to her, he perched down on top of it between the inkwells. He didn't speak until she sat down behind the desk facing him. "I noticed from the window that she was making life difficult for you again," he said, his alert grey eyes meeting hers. "I think I know what brought this on. That's what I came to tell you."

"I'm not sure that I'm interested anymore. I've had enough," she said dejectedly.

"Don't let her get to you. The inspector's report came today. I managed to get a look at it when she was out of the class; the time she was ticking you off. Anyhow, your class got the highest praise."

"Thank you John. You have lifted my spirits from an all-time low but I still don't know if I can carry on here. She hates me so much that it frightens me. She's determined to be rid of me it seems." Then smiling, she looked down at him again, and said, "I'm delighted that my efforts have been recognised by someone at least. Thanks again for telling me."

Getting up from the desk, he walked to the door. Looking back at her again, he said, "Don't let her get the better of you. You are a great teacher." He was gone before she had time to reply.

Back in her lodgings, Mary Kate lay down on the bed. She felt more gloomy and downhearted than she had done in a long time. Not even the news about the inspector's report lifted her spirits. Argue with herself as she might, she felt lonely and depressed; but she admitted that she was a good teacher.

The distant jingle of the dinner-bell sounded, and trembled away into silence. She rose from the bed and went over to the mirror above the washstand. She combed her curly auburn hair roughly, before pinning it back at the nape of her neck. She gazed at her reflection quietly; the large soft brown eyes stared back gloomily. "Your countenance looks as sorrowful as a stricken deer," James Thompson would always say when she was in a bad mood. Remembering this made her smile, and then she laughed shortly and scornfully at herself before leaving the dreary room and going downstairs.

If she hoped that supper would lift her spirits she was to be disappointed, as the same watery cabbage and fatty bacon was placed in front of her. Staring at the unappetising food, she remembered her grandmother's delicious cooking and wished again that she were back home.

As she was about to leave the dining-room the landlady called after her, "Mary Kate. A letter came for you today." Taking the buff-coloured envelope, she went back to her room and opened it. She read it over and over again "an interview for the teaching post in Ballyneely National School," she repeated aloud. 'And I had almost forgotten that I had applied. Clutching the envelope to her chest, she swung around in a circle. Then sitting down on the bed she reminded herself that it was only an interview after all. But even if she didn't get the post, she would have a weekend at home. This thought alone sent her spirits soaring. Sitting down on the bed again, she began to write a letter to her grandmother.

When she had finished the letter, the early high spirits had subsided, leaving that special cupboard of distant memory. The same Parish Priest that her grandmother had shown contempt of would be on the interview panel. "Am I forgetting the narrow minds of that small rural community?" she asked herself, as Wee Sally O'Neil's words came back to haunt her. "You're a bastard. You have no Daddy. And your Ma was sent to America," she had screeched spitefully.

Although Mary Kate couldn't understand what 'bastard' meant back then, she had understood that it was something to feel shame about. She remembered now, how she had ran to the far corner of the playground and hid behind a tree.

The pride she had felt about the two pennies the teacher had given her earlier for having all her spellings correct now vanished.

She now recalled not telling her grandmother and instead had confided in the old lady at the Rectory that she called Aunt Jean. She knew now that Aunt Jean was James Thompson's aunt and not hers.

Her memory of her was one of love and kindness and a wisdom that only time could bring. Jean had held her close and comforted her with wise words that restored her confidence and self-esteem.

She smiled to herself as she remembered taking the photograph of herself, her mother Maura and her New York husband, Andrew Jefferson to school the following day.

Seated beside Sally O'Neill the following day, she showed her the photograph. "That's my Mammy and Daddy and me. It was taken here in Clougher when I was four," she added, waiting for her reaction.

For a brief moment she looked lost for words. "Well ... why are you not living with them then? Everybody else lives with their mother and father." "Anyway," she went on. "He's not your real Daddy."

"Aye, he is. And they wanted me to go to America with them. But I didn't want to leave Granny, and Auntie Jean, an' James Thompson and Molly," she finished breathlessly.

"What's going on here?" Miss Donnelly angry voice made them jump.

Picking up the photograph and looking at it briefly, she continued.

"You are here to concentrate on your lessons, not look at photographs. Why did you take this photograph to school Mary Kate?"

Feeling her face redden, she stammered. "I wanted to show it to Sally ... she needed to see my Daddy."

"She's telling lies, Miss. He's not her Daddy. She has no Daddy."

Clearing her throat Miss Donnelly replied angrily. "If you attended to your work, Sally, as much as you do to matters that don't concern you, we'd all be better off. Put the photograph of your parents carefully back in your bag, Mary Kate, and we can continue the lesson."

The following day Miss Donnelly caught up with Mary Kate on her way home from school. Getting off her bicycle, she said. "I've been waiting for a chance to have a word with you about that episode with Sally and the photograph." Mary Kate looked at her teacher with apprehension. "I'm not going to scold you. I just want to give you a little advice. Don't let anyone annoy you in that way again. You are a clever, bright pupil and you have a family to be proud of. If Sally, or anyone else for that matter, asks you personal questions again, don't answer them. Just smile." She gazed at the distant hills for a moment before she spoke again. "Take this advice from someone who knows Mary Kate." Smiling down at her, she laid her hand lightly on her head. "You have so much to be proud of. Don't forget that."

As she cycled away, Mary Kate felt full of admiration for Miss Donnelly and her words of advice made her heart feel light again. Looking back, she knew that it was in that instant, that she knew she wanted to be a teacher.

Looking again at the letter, Aunt Jean's face came before her "Courage Mary Kate. Give it your best shot," her voice seemed to come out of the mists of memory. Picking up the letter, she left the room.

Chapter 2

Old Ghosts

Father Connor McLaughlin sat in his study pondering the following day's duty. The interview and appointment of the new teacher for the school was much on his mind as he read again, the letters from the applicants for interview.

His brow knotted into a set of wrinkles as he tried to remember why he should have some recollection of Mary Kate Quinn. Something from the past was lodged in his mind. Try as he might, he just couldn't remember what it was. "Old age is a menace. A menace," he repeatedly whispered. There were many days when he just wanted the burden of ministry lifted from him. He stared out the window, lost in thought, when he spied Eleanor Donnelly making her way slowly from the Church gates. "Ah, she will know about the applicants. The very one," he whispered to himself, as he hurried from the room.

At the driveway gates he managed to attract her attention.

"Wondered if you might help me with something. Would you have half an hour to spare?"

"Time is the one thing I have plenty of Father."

They both shuffled up the driveway towards the house in silence.

Seated opposite him in his study, Eleanor asked. "How can I help you Father?"

"It's about the new teacher applicants. There are three applications. One man in his fifties, another woman from the Grange School ... said to be a holy terror, and Mary Kate Quinn. That's what I wanted to ask you about. Something about the name rings a bell but I just can't remember what it is."

The steady grey eyes that met hers had a quizzical expression.

"I taught Mary Kate at Ballyneely up until she went to College. She was one of the best students I ever had. A grand girl. Sara did a good job in bringing her up."

"Now it's come back to me. Didn't Sara leave her husband to go and live with that man ... what's his name?"

"James Thompson," Eleanor filled in. "No Father. She didn't go and live with him … in the way I think you might be implying. She went to work for him.

You see, I know because Molly Sheehy was my old neighbour and also worked at the Rectory."

Putting his hands up, he said. "Hold it there. I wasn't implying anything. It's just that this matter was brought to my notice many years ago by a couple of the parishioners. Anyhow, I felt at the time it was my duty to ask Sara if there was any truth in the rumours."

"And," Eleanor prompted.

"She told me her side of the story. But I did have to remind her that her duty lay with the man she had married."

"She had no option. Believe me, she had no option. Sara married John Quinn when she was eighteen years old. He was quite a bit older. Anyhow, they farmed together and it was a hard, grinding life. Sara was always a great worker.

Then they had a daughter named Maura. When Maura was just fourteen she was … how can … I say it? Molested. Raped repeatedly by her father's first cousin and nearest neighbour."

She watched as Father Connor blessed himself, a shocked expression on his face. "Continue," he said, with a slight nod.

"Well, Sara only found out when it was discovered that Maura was pregnant. When she told John he ranted and raved. Just refused to believe that his cousin was responsible. So he sent Maura to the convent and instructed the nuns to put the baby in their orphanage. Then he produced a one way ticket for his daughter's passage to New York. Sara only found out what he intended when the receipt from the shipping company fell out of his overcoat pocket when she was hanging it up. She was to sail that very day, so she managed to make her way to the quayside in time to say goodbye. Anyway, she promised her daughter that she would look after Mary Kate until she returned. You see ... the nuns had a tight grip of poor Maura. They were determined to follow John Quinn's instructions and there was no escape."

Father Connor sighed deeply before he spoke again. "Did Maura Quinn want to keep the baby? And how did Sara end up at the Rectory?

"Aye, she wanted to keep the baby. The nuns let her feed the infant for the first few days and mother love just took over. Then the baby was taken away from her and she was only told on the same day that she was going to New York ... never to return. Poor girl, she even contemplated jumping overboard a few days out to sea. Sara somehow managed to persuade the nuns that her husband had changed his mind about Mary Kate being brought up in the orphanage. She had to lie to keep her promise. Well, she ended up going to the old Rectory where she had once worked. Molly Sheehy had been a good friend to her when she had worked there. But it was a different place from the one she remembered. Poor Molly was crippled with Rheumatism and James Thompson was an alcoholic. The house was a damp, miserable shambles. But Sara Quinn was a strong woman and she transformed the lives of Molly, James Thompson, and his elderly aunt, Jean. And she did a grand job at bringing up Mary Kate. They all did."

The housekeeper, carrying a tray of tea and scones interrupted them.

When they had finished their tea, Father Connor asked, "What happened to John and the cousin?"

"When Mary Kate was about four, John discovered that his cousin Seamus had been … interfering with another wee girl. A close neighbour. I'm not too sure about the details. Anyhow, it made him realise that Sara had been telling the truth. He tried to kill Seamus. It seems he would have killed him if he had been able to find cartridges for the gun he had. But, he did manage to scare him. Anyway, he left and emigrated.

John came to the Rectory shortly after that when he knew he was dying. Sara took him in and nursed him to the end."

Father Connor sighed deeply and stared out the window in silence. "It's a sad tale. A very sad tale."

"Remember Father … this was told to me in the strictest confidence. Nobody knows about it except for the family and the mother of the other wee girl.

The one thing Sara always wanted to protect Mary Kate from … was the knowledge that her father was a rapist."

"Thanks for telling me all this Eleanor."

Eleanor met his steady gaze for a few seconds before speaking again. "You wanted my opinion. Well, here it is. Mary Kate would make a fine teacher for Ballyneely School. Now I'll be on my way."

When she had gone, he sat silently pondering on the story she had told him. He thought he was beyond being saddened and shocked by man's injustice to man and yet he was stunned by this revelation. Still, he reminded himself that he must judge each applicant on his or her merit.

A few days later, while shopping in the village, Eleanor accidentally overheard the news about Seamus Quinn's old house undergoing restoration and she instantly knew what this would mean to Sara. She would have to go and see her. She must tell her about the possibility of Mary Kate's appointment to the Ballyneely School post. Now she was beginning to doubt her wisdom about telling Father Connor, because she knew now that Sara wouldn't want Mary Kate back in Ballyneely, if Seamus Quinn were anywhere near.

Walking slowly along the driveway that led to the Rectory, Eleanor hoped that Sara would be alone. Mist hung heavily around the old house, the distant cry of seagulls and the almost silent plod of horses' hooves as they pulled the plough in a nearby field gave the place a feeling of eeriness. Molly's descriptions of the old Rectory had made Eleanor feel that she knew every stick and stone long before she first visited the place.

Sara answered her knock, "Eleanor, how lovely to see you. Come in, come in she said, with a broad smile of welcome. In the kitchen, Sara busied herself with making tea and as Eleanor told her about the teaching post and how Mary Kate would be fairly likely to get the job, much to Eleanor's surprise, Sara beamed with delight.

Eleanor made an instant decision to keep quiet about Seamus Quinn "She will know in time enough," she reasoned.

Sara carried a tray of tea and scones into the drawing-room and they settled down to talk about old times. It was the memories of Molly that brought the distant and painful past back into Eleanor's mind.

Piling memory on memory, Eleanor Donnelly told Sara the entire story of her own life.

Chapter 3

Eleanor's Story

Childhood memory for Eleanor, was mixed up in her head to a point where she couldn't quite remember which parts really happened and which she invented. Whispered comments only half understood left her feeling insecure, lonely and unhappy during those growing years. She would wander down to the old Oak tree in the meadow and sit down between its craggy roots and listen to the breeze rustle the leaves high above her head. This had always been her private place, a hideout where she could contemplate her thoughts.

She had tried down the years to block out the most

painful parts, and it was only now that she wanted desperately to understand her past and maybe through understanding, forgive.

Eleanor's memories of the house and the man she had called her father were anything but happy ones. It took the best part of forty years to come to an acceptance about the truth of her beginnings and the ruined lives left in its wake. Perhaps that was why she had identified so much with Mary Kate.

Looking back now, she could not say that the man she thought of as her father was cruel to her. Dan McGarth had simply ignored her very existence. In early childhood, she remembered trying to grab his attention; she so desperately wanted his approval, just to be noticed. As the years passed, she had given up trying and withdrew into her own private world of make believe. When Molly Sheehy told her the story of Sara and Mary Kate, she had wished that her own mother could have shared Sara's courage.

As she stared at the stone wall in front of the house, old half-forgotten memories seemed to whisper to her across time. The grey-stone house from where she stood, looked a picture of middle-class rural respectability, just like the soft charms Dan McGrath showed to the outside world, which hid the true nature of their existence within.

She remembered the day she came home early from school with the toothache and found the strange man talking to her mother, Jane in the kitchen.

The stranger was tall with grey hair, and grey sideburns and spoke with a strange sounding accent. She watched unobserved from the clink in the door. Her mother's face, pale as death and full of fear, was urging the stranger to go.

"If he finds you here they'll be more hell to pay. I have it tough enough as it is.

If I'd produced a son for him ... he might have been a bit easier on me."

"Is he unkind to my granddaughter?"

"No. He just ignores her. But I make up for that. She gets all the love from me that she needs. She's all I have."

"The bruises on your face. Did he do that?"

She nodded. "It's nothing ... I've had worse ... I'm used to it."

"Nobody should have to put up with that. My mother should have told me at the time. She only told me the day before she died. When James was killed in action it broke our hearts. And then Annie died of consumption and her only child died of the same disease the following spring."

Jane sighed deeply before she spoke again. "I'm sorry. It seems we were all doomed to heartbreak. Poor fool me ... I fell in love with James. And when my condition was found out, your mother sent me packing. A common slut of a servant, she called me. Even now I wonder why I was so stupid and naive."

"Why did you marry that man?"

"My father arranged it. Paid him with the three-hundred pounds your mother gave him to keep my mouth shut. He just wanted an un-paid skivvy and a family of sons of his own … and the three-hundred pounds."

"Could you not get away from him?"

"I was going to run away a time or two. Thought of Canada. But he's taken all the spirit out of me now. And it's just too late."

Moving closer to where she stood, he put a hand on her shoulder. From her secret position at the door, Eleanor thought he was about to strike her; this was what her father did regularly in her presence, and in her naivety she thought that this is what all men did. But when he spoke again, his voice was gentle, "It's never too late. I could find a place for you both to live. I'm not a wealthy man. But I have enough, more than enough. And I owe you. My son was a coward … and my mother a high-minded bully. And you have suffered greatly because of it."

"If we left, he'd find us wherever we went. He would hate to lose his possessions. That's the way he'd see it. Now you better go."

"Before I go, I want to set up a trust fund for Eleanor in the bank. For her education and for her needs."

Jane put up her hand, "He'd find out and I wouldn't be able to use it."

"No. Listen. No information or mail will ever come

here. You just have to go to the bank whenever you need it. He needn't know."

"I hardly ever get out of here. I don't see how I could even get as far as the bank ... without being half-killed."

"You'll find some way." He handed her an envelope, "In here you'll find the details. Guard it well."

"Now go ... for God's sake, go."

From her hiding place, Eleanor watched him go with a mixture of confusion and hope. Her mother jumped in surprise when she went into the kitchen a couple of minutes later. "What are you doing home? Did you see anything?" she screeched, grabbing her by the arms. Eleanor shook her head vigorously, "No, no I saw nothing. I come home early with the toothache." Gradually, her mother loosened her grip and the crazed look left her face.

Eleanor wanted to know more about the strange man. She wanted to ask a dozen questions. But she was afraid, afraid of her mother in this strange state of fear and panic. So, instead, she pondered alone on all that she had seen and heard and endured as best she could, her lonely, silent existence.

She was eight years old when her father was called away as a juror to a court case in Dublin. It was the first time in her life that he had ever been away from the farm and the sheer pleasure of his absence brought a light-hearted feeling to both their lives.

Before his departure, he left instructions about all the work that had to be done in his absence. "If you leave the house, even for an hour … I'll know, and I don't need to tell you of the consequences," he said, with blood curdling menace in his tone.

As they watched him go, Jane said quietly, "Fancy being judged by him. Pillar of society, some think. But we know better. Aye … to our sorrow. We know better."

Her mother wakened Eleanor, early the following morning. "You're not going to school today. I want you to help me with the milking first, and then I want you to go down to Brennan's and tell young Johnny that I want to see him."

"Where are we going?"

"Don't ask questions, just do as I say. And when I have to tell a lie or two, keep your mouth shut. Firmly shut. Do you hear me?" she asked urgently between clenched teeth.

When Johnny arrived, Jane told him that she was sick and had to go to see the doctor in the town. "If I'm not back before milking time will you do it for me?" she asked, "I'll give you five shillings and get you a packet of cigarettes if you promise not to breathe a word."

"Not a word. I promise," he said eagerly, smiling in anticipation. As a servant boy, Johnny was eager to earn a bit extra money and she knew that his half yearly pay was a long way off.

They walked to the station in silence, Eleanor not daring to ask where they were going.

The town was busy when they arrived. Eleanor watched the mass of people wander around narrow streets, horses pulled loaded carts towards the market and above the commotion she could hear a fiddler playing a lively tune.

At the bank door her mother gave her a tug, "Stop staring and come on," she urged. She looked around fearfully before going in. "Stand here and don't move," she commanded, before going over to the counter.

Eventually, after much explaining, the clerk handed her some bank notes.

Outside, Jane looked around her from the shadows of the doorway, with that fearful expression that Eleanor had come to know so well.

"Across the road, quick," she urged, as they half ran into a drapery shop.

Ushering Eleanor in front of her, she hastily chose two sets of school clothing and a grey coat for her.

"And I want a pair of black boots, size four I think. Could you hurry, I don't want to miss the train," she added breathlessly. Eleanor wanted to stay in the shop and look at the beautiful clothing, but she was ushered out as soon as the items were paid for.

As they briskly walked along the street, Eleanor

wished with all her heart that she could stay in the town and mingle with the people who laughed and talked in light-hearted voices, she wanted to be normal and unafraid, at least for one day.

Then she saw him step down from a trap and tie the pony to a rail. It was the man she saw in the kitchen talking to her mother on the day she had toothache. Her mother was about to hurry passed when he ran after them and called her name. "Jane, wait. I'm glad to see you again. And this must be wee Eleanor."

Bending down he looked at her. He saw a slight figure in grey, with a hand-knit grey shawl wrapped close to a tiny waist. From under the brim of her bonnet two great dark brown eyes gazed at him, and a curling strand of hair, a rich chestnut brown, was blown by the breeze.

With a pained expression in his eyes he spoke softly, "Annie. It's like looking at Annie all over again. I'm a boy again, back in the nursery at Craigallan."

As she looked into his eyes, Eleanor could see them mist over with tears.

Then in a broken voice he said, "I'm John Henderson, an old friend of your mother's. She err ... worked for my family long ago." Then he held out his hand, and she took it and felt the warmth of his gentle, firm handshake.

"We must get going. I have to get back to the farm." Not taking his eyes from Eleanor's face he said, "Please take her to see me. Please try and find a way."

"I doubt it. Just got out today because he's gone to Dublin. He could come back at any minute."

"I know. But there must be a way."

"No way. Getting out today was nothing short of a miracle."

Glancing at the shop behind him he asked, "Would you like that doll that's in the window?"

Eleanor found herself nodding vigorously, as her eyes caught sight of the beautiful doll with blue eyes wearing a red frock.

"I won't be a minute," he said as he almost ran into the shop.

Jane sighed, "I wish to God he wouldn't buy that. It will be something else to hide. Only more bother." Then turning Eleanor around to face her she said, "If he ever sees it … say granny bought it. And don't ever say you met this man or that we were here."

"I'll never say a word. I promise."

"You better stick to that or I'll pay a heavy price for this day."

"It'll be all right Mammy. Nobody will ever know."

A couple of minutes later, he handed her the doll and a brown bag filled with sweets. "Thank you," she said quietly.

"You are most welcome." Then bending down close to her face, he kissed her lightly on the cheek, "If you ever need anything come to see me. I'll be there for you as long as I'm spared."

"We better get going," her mother's urgent voice

broke the poignant moment.

When they had walked a few paces, Eleanor looked back at him. He was still standing in the same place staring after them, he smiled and she smiled back.

On the train journey Eleanor cradled her doll closely unable to believe her luck, but her thoughts were with the stranger back in the town. She repeated his name over and over, "John Henderson. Craigallan", so determined was she, not to forget. Bits of the conversation she had heard between him and her mother kept coming back. Finally she ventured,
 "Who was that man Mammy?"
 "Don't you ever ask me that again. Don't ever mention his name even. Do you hear me?" she almost screamed, anger and fear blazing in her eyes.
"And hide that as soon as we get off the train," she added, pointing to the doll.
 Eleanor felt anger at her mother's refusal to tell her anything, the earlier gratitude for the clothes and the visit to town suddenly evaporated.
Her thoughts went back to her eavesdropping that day and she knew that the money her mother got from the bank had come from the stranger. As she recalled the conversation again it suddenly occurred to her that if she was his granddaughter, he must be her grandfather. But her grandfather was dead.
The confusion went round, and round, in her head as

the train wound its way between the dark hills.

Chapter 4

The Enlightening

During the next two years a growing sense of loneliness seemed to envelope Eleanor, making her more silent than ever, and at night she would rescue her beloved doll from its hiding place. She had secretly vowed to herself that she would find John Henderson at this place named Craigallan and find out if he really was her grandfather.

Johnny was standing at the back door when she came home from school.

"What's wrong?" she asked, noting the look of alarm on his face.

"It's Dan. Your father … he was hit by the horse on the head."

"Is he dead?" she asked.

"Maybe I shouldn't be the one that tells you. But aye, I think he is."

Inside the kitchen the neighbours had gathered and her mother sat staring into space near the fire. Going over to her, Eleanor touched her arm, "Oh, its you. Did you hear what happened?" she said, with a dazed expression.

"He's dead Eleanor. He's dead," she repeated, as though she was convincing herself of the fact.

"I know, Johnny told me."

"The horse kicked him in the head in the stable. Just flung out and killed him," she ended in a sigh.

Eleanor found herself surrounded by people with concerned expressions on their faces, offering tea and sympathy.

"Poor wee soul. Such a shock for her," they sighed.

But Eleanor felt nothing - no emotion, no sadness - just a feeling of bewilderment. It dawned on her that she was supposed to cry, but try as she might no tears would come.

During the three-day wake Eleanor listened to bits of conversation between the people who called. They would shake their heads sympathetically at her and say, "Poor wee thing, losing her father. He was a decent man - always willing to help out a neighbour." Eleanor wanted to shout back, "He was no decent man. We lived in terror of him." Instead she kept silent and stole away to her room. She would lift her doll from the bed and hold her close, "I won't have to hide you anymore. He's gone and he won't be back."

On the evening before the funeral Eleanor left the smoke-filled, oppressive kitchen and went out to the barn. Sitting on a bale of straw, she listened to the people come and go. From amongst the voices that filtered through her consciousness, came one she recognised. Mary Sheehy, and her daughter Molly, were regular visitors to the farm and as they talked together in the quiet stillness just outside the barn door, she pulled herself up on the hay and strained to hear what was being said.

"I can't take any more of this 'decent man' bit," Mary was saying, "I seen the bruises on her many a time. The poor woman, she had a rough time of it."

"What about wee Eleanor. Was he cruel to her?"

"I don't think she suffered any blows. But he was mentally bad to her too. What a price to pay for being born on the right side of the blanket. She would have been better to have brought her up on her own, illegitimate or not … than that."

As the voices moved away and faded, Eleanor fell back into the darkness, where she murmured over and over again, "illegitimate. Right side of the blanket." Her mind filled with confusion and she vowed again, to find out the truth about her beginnings.

When the funeral was over Jane threw herself wholeheartedly into the work on the farm and for Eleanor, life went back almost to the way it had been before, only now she had an endless list of farmyard chores to do before and after school. She was glad to be freed from the fear that Dan had instilled in her over the years. Looking back, she recoiled at the memory of his thick freckled hands, the hard compact strength of them, and the way the sweat broke out in a fine glistening line along the knuckles when he was angry, and the hateful words falling from his mocking mouth like poisoned honey. If she expected her mother to break out in song because of her new freedom from fear, she was to be disappointed. The pride she had felt in openly wearing her new school clothes and coat, and playing with her doll in the kitchen had helped to dispel the disappointment a little. But she hated the farm chores and longed for her mother just to pay a little attention to her.

A few days later, Eleanor found her mother crying in the kitchen and clutching a brown envelope. "He has shamed me. Even in death ... he has shamed me. Left the farm to Manny," she said, brokenly.
"Does that mean we have to live someplace else?"
"The will says I can live on here for my day and have a wee bit of rent for the two wee fields at Cruck," she

ended, before breaking into uncontrollable sobs.

Unable to comfort her, Eleanor went upstairs to her room and threw herself down on the bed. She lay silently staring at the cracks in the ceiling, her thoughts on her mother's misery at the loss of the farm. The more she thought about it, the more pleased she bccamc at no longer being a slave to the farm. She had watched her mother count the money he had hidden under the floorboards and knew that it contained many rolls of banknotes. With that, and the money the stranger left in the bank, Eleanor knew that she could manage.

As she lay listening to the whistling autumn wind the realisation that she was really on her own, struck her forcibly.

On the following morning Eleanor rushed through the milking and calf feeding, before washing and dressing carefully.

"I'm off to school now Mammy," she called to her mother from the milk-room door. She heard her mutter a goodbye, before she set off.

At the end of the lane she turned towards the village, her hand gripping the money she had taken from Dan's black box that lay under her mother's bed.

She doubted if she would miss it, and anyway she felt that she had no option.

At the crossroads, she looked warily around her and quickly hid her schoolbag under the hawthorn hedge. On the train journey she felt anxious, she had never before travelled anywhere alone. In the town she looked around, and then went into the hardware shop to seek directions. An elderly man in a brown coat asked, "Can I help you?"

"Aye. I'm looking for directions to Craigallan"

"No place I've ever heard tell of."

"A man called Henderson lives there. John Henderson," she said, with sinking spirits.

"Ah, now I got you. Craigallan's not the name of a place. It's the name of a house. Only one of them Henderson's left I heard. They were riding the rigging high at one day. But their day's nearly done. And what would a wee girl like you be wanting with him?"

"Oh, just a message for him. Now, could you tell me how to find the place?"

"Aye, it's about two miles away."

When she got the directions she set off at a brisk pace along the coast road until she reached Ballyhillon village and then following the directions she walked up the hill and along the high stone wall until she reached the big iron gates that heralded the imposing entrance to Craigallan House.

The driveway was long and shaded with beech trees on either side. Her steps slowed and she licked her dry lips nervously as the big grey house came into view. She climbed the stone steps, rang the bell and listened as it trembled away into the distance. Finally, with much rustling from within, the door was opened by an old woman in a white apron who peered at her suspiciously.

"I want to talk to Mr Henderson. I've come a long way," she added nervously.

"And who might you be?"

"I'm Eleanor McGrath."

"Well, you'll have to come back some other time. Mr Henderson's not well. Not up to visitors."

Eleanor saw the door begin to close on her, and with a note of desperation in her voice she said, "Please … please. He'll want to see me for he's my grandfather. He told me so."

She saw a look of stunned surprise come into the old woman's eyes as she slowly opened the big door again.

"Stand here till I go and see what he says. And don't move," she added, before shuffling off into the dimness within.

After what seemed an age, she came back into view and nodded, "He'll see you.

But don't stay long for he's not well."

Eleanor followed her into the big hall where she opened a door to the left.

He sat in big chair close to an open fire. The room was lined with books and smelled of beeswax and burning timber from the fire. She stood awkwardly by the door until he looked around and saw her. Getting up from his chair he smiled at her, "Welcome. I'm glad to see you. Is your mother with you?"

"She doesn't know I'm here."

"Oh, I see. She'll have a search party out when she finds you missing."

"Not if I get home before school-time."

"I read about Dan's - your father's death in the paper. I'm sorry," he added, with a sympathetic nod.

"I didn't cry or anything. Mammy didn't cry either."

"I see." Clearing his throat loudly, he glanced at the old woman standing in the doorway, "It's all right, Maggie. I'll call if I need you."

"Don't tire yourself. You know what the doctor said. I've already told her not to be staying long," she said, with a note of annoyance.

"I'll call if I need you." Eventually, they heard the door close, and her mutterings of displeasure faded into the distance.

"She means well. She has been in this house since she was a girl."

"Why did she come as a girl?"

"She came as a maid in the beginning. Then she was the cook. That was in our heyday. Anyhow, she means well. What brought you here on your own? Mind you, I'm delighted to see you. But I wish your mother had come with you."

"She wouldn't come. She just cries all the time because he didn't leave her the farm. And I had to ask you something."

He rubbed his chin slowly, with a puzzled expression.

"I'll answer your questions - if it's possible. What has your mother told you about me?"

"Nothing. But I know you're my grandfather, for I heard you say it."

"Oh, when was that?"

"The day you were at our house. I ... I was listening behind the kitchen door." She licked her dry lips, and looked at the ground before going on. "I come home that day with the toothache. And you were in the kitchen. So I listened behind the door."

When she looked up she saw tenderness in his blue-grey eyes, such as she had never experienced before. "Go on tell me what you heard, and what you didn't understand."

"I only understood a wee bit of what you said. You said you were my grandfather and that James was dead."

Turning away, he reached for the poker and idly poked the fire for a few seconds before he spoke, "I can see that I owe you an explanation. I owe you the truth about the past. I just wish your mother had told you. It's her place more than mine." He sighed deeply before he spoke again. "Your mother worked here as a nanny to my sister's child when she was a young girl.

At that time, I lived in Belfast with my wife and son, James. We spent our summers here at Craigallan with my mother. Anyhow, James and your mother became friends ... more than friends. They fell in love and as a result of this you came to be. James was a student in London at this time and your mother discovered that you were on the way after he left here for his final year in College. She wrote and told him about you. A tram killed him six weeks after his summer here. We were all heartbroken, our lives in tatters. He was our only child.

So your mother was left with you on the way and no support. I didn't know anything about it at the time. My mother knew and chose to keep it to herself. She was a snob you see Eleanor, and thought that a servant girl was not good enough for her grandson. So she dismissed your mother from the house and a marriage was arranged for her with Dan, the man you thought of as your father."

"So I wouldn't be born on the wrong side of the blanket."

"Where did you hear that?" he asked, with a note of surprise in his voice.

"At the time of the wake, I overheard our neighbour, Mary Sheehy say that to her daughter Molly. I wasn't sure what she meant, but I think I do now."

"You're a perceptive wee girl," he said, as a hint of a smile formed on his lips.

"Like I was saying, I only found out about your existence a few years ago when my mother was dying. I can't forgive her for keeping this from me. You are all I have left of James. She had no right. In the beginning when I found out about you, I thought that James had bowed out of his responsibilities. Had left your mother to face things alone. Then three weeks ago I made a discovery. Am I going too fast for you?" he suddenly asked.

"No, no. I want to know everything."

"Good. Well, getting back to the discovery. You see I'm selling this house to a cousin. It's too big for me and too costly to keep up. Well, workmen were clearing out the old beds from the attic rooms, used to be where the servants slept. Anyhow, as they were about to burn one of the mattresses a letter addressed to the old cook fell out. They brought it to me and I found a letter from James, your father that had been sent to the cook for your mother. It hadn't even been opened. I read it, and in the letter he told your mother that they would get married as soon as he finished college and they would immigrate to Canada where they could bring up their child in peace. Your mother never saw the letter. I was going to see her and show it to her two weeks ago. But, I developed pneumonia and had to put it off. Then you turn up out of the blue." As she looked at his quiet countenance and gentle eyes, she felt the huge weight of uncertainty lift from her shoulders and she smiled, "Thank you for telling me grandfather," she added, quietly.

Reaching out, he took her small hand and held it between his big ones, "I'm so glad you came, so very glad. And I'll be moving closer to you in a few weeks. I own a house at Creega Port that used to be an old hunting lodge, so you will be within walking distance of me. We have a lot more to talk about, but I think that's enough for one day, eh? Now you must get a bit of lunch if you are to get back in time. And while Maggie gets it ready you can have a quick look around the old house. The nursery is at the top of the house. Thought you might like to see where your father spent his early years and where your mother worked. She wandered around the large rooms and in the nursery she sat on the dusty rocking horse, burying her face in its tangled mane as she rocked to and fro. His voice coming from the doorway startled her, "I see you've found the old horse. I played on it in my time and so did your father. It's rightfully yours now, and anything else that takes your fancy for that matter."

"Thank you, I'd love it always - like the doll."

"Do you still have the doll?"

She nodded. "I'll always keep the doll."

Along the driveway Eleanor looked up at the sun shining through the russet-coloured autumn leaves and felt joy at being alive. At last she knew who she was and would no longer skulk in the shadows as she felt the first fluttering of joy stir her heart. She felt strangely close to the father she had never met and the feeling of belonging brought sheer delight to her heart as she skipped along with noiseless feet under the shade of the trees.

She picked up her schoolbag from under the hedge and walked home. Her mother hardly noticed her entrance into the kitchen, "When you have eaten your dinner, there's work to be done," she said, without looking at her.

"I'll work for a couple of hours. Then I must do my homework."

"The farm's more important than the schoolwork."

"No it's not, for it's not yours anymore."

The blow to the side of her face sent her reeling backward on the chair, sending her sprawling to the ground. "Don't you give me any more cheek," her mother's angry voice screamed, as she scrambled to her feet, tears welling up in her eyes. "Why did you do that? I was only telling you the truth."

"The farm's our living, and don't you forget it girl. I'll fight for what's rightfully mine. He won't put a foot on the place. I suffered for years for this farm and nobody's taking it from me - do you hear me?" The look of hate in her eyes frightened Eleanor as she tried to reason with her.

"But if I do well at school, I could maybe be a teacher and earn us a living that way. I hate this old farm just like I hated him. I hate it - I hate it," she sobbed uncontrollably.

"Hate it or not, this is where we stay. And you will do your share." The determination in her voice made Eleanor realise that she was beyond reason and when she spoke again the fire had gone out of her tone.

"All right. I'll help you. But please let me have time to do my schoolwork too."

Eleanor waited for a response from her mother, but

none came. Instead she stood staring into space with a look of desperation. Suddenly, she began to cry, her shoulders shaking with sobs.

Taking Eleanor in her arms, she gently smoothed her hair, "Eleanor, my poor wee waif. I'm sorry. I'm sorry," she repeated. "I of all people shouldn't have done that. For I know what it's like to be on the receiving end. Oh God, what am I coming to. He did this to me.

Even in death he punishes me. I'm only twenty-nine years old and I feel like I'm ninety-nine. Owning the farm would have given us a wee bit of security and left me with a wee bit of self-respect. Now I have nothing."

Seeing the tragic look on her face, Eleanor began, "Mammy, it's all right. I love you and my daddy loved you."

"He didn't even like me. Sure you of all people should know that. You saw what he did to me."

"I don't mean him. I mean my real daddy, James Henderson."

"How do you know about - him?" she asked in a near whisper, grabbing her by the shoulders she bent down until they made eye contact.

Suddenly afraid, Eleanor licked her dry lips, "I heard everything you both ... said that day that my grandfather was here. I came home with toothache. I always knew that - he, Dan, wasn't my father. He hated me like he hated you."

"Who told you about James?"

"I heard things said at the wake about me nearly being on the wrong side of the blanket.

Anyway, I went to see my grandfather and I told him what I heard. Then he said I had a right to know. So he told me. And he told me about a letter that James had sent to you before he was killed. He only found it the other day in the cook's old mattress. He said in the letter that the two of you would get married and go to live in Canada where you could bring me up in peace. My grandfather says he is coming to give it to you."

She saw the colour drain from her mother's face as she stared at her in stunned silence. Then she loosened the tight grip on Eleanor's shoulders and staggered to a chair.

It seemed like an age before she spoke again.

"My God, I can't believe that you know. Know more than me."

Going over to where she sat, she nervously put an arm on her mother's shoulder. "Please don't be mad at him for telling me. He said it would be better coming from you. But he had to tell me because I knew most of it already."

"Go up and play with your doll for a while. Go on. I need to be on my own for a bit."

From the doorway Eleanor asked, "Are you mad with me for finding out?"

As she waited for a response she heard her sigh deeply,

Secrets on the Breeze

"I don't know. I just don't know."

A week later, Eleanor came home from school and found Mary Sheehy in deep conversation with her mother in the kitchen. A letter sat on the table beside them. When the conversation turned suddenly to the weather, Eleanor knew that what was being discussed was not for her ears.

They looked up as she went in, and in a glance Eleanor could tell that her mother had been crying.

When they both smiled at her, Eleanor felt relief rush through her.

When she had gone Jane said, "Sit yourself down. I have something to tell you. The letter you told me about came in the post. Seems he's not well enough to come and see me yet. So just in case something would happen to him, he posted it." She silently gazed out the window with a wishful expression before she spoke again. "It could have all been so different, if only I'd known - I wouldn't have hated myself so much."

"But it's all in the past, I suppose. I told Mary everything and she's the only one, apart from us, that must ever know. So no telling anything at school. It's our secret." Eleanor nodded. "You can have more time to do your homework. I've not decided what to do about Manny and the farm yet. I could fight it in law. But … it might let out a can of worms about the past. But I'll not tell him that - let him sweat it out."

"Can I go and see Mr Henderson - grandfather sometimes?"

"Oh, I don't know. People might talk and it might affect my chances of getting the farm."

"But no one needs to know where I'm going. Please. He's old and sick, and he wants to see me an odd time and he's giving me the old rocking horse." She waited patiently for a response, her heart thundering nervously.

"I'll think about it. But no more sneaking off for I'll know. And I don't want you bringing the rocking horse here. People would only be asking questions. You can go to see him the odd time on the quiet and play with it there."

As Eleanor grew up, the battle for ownership of the farm continued. Each time Manny appeared in the yard a new battle would begin. Solicitors' letters with threats to contest the will went back and forth with no final conclusion in sight.

Eleanor visited her grandfather in his new home as often as she could and it was his care and guidance that saw her through the dark days of conflict and uncertainty at home. He taught her to treasure books and encouraged and helped her with her school-work. Before leaving she would go to the special room he had set aside for her to play with the toys that her ancestors had treasured, while she dared to dream of happier days ahead.

Secrets on the Breeze

Sometimes at night she would steal out of her room and go to Mary Sheehy's house and it was to Mary that she could give utterance to her darkest fears about the conflict at home.

"I wish for her own sake and for yours that she would let him have the oul' farm. She would get enough to do her without. But her pride comes into it you see," Mary would say, as she made their cocoa. Sometimes Mary's daughter Molly would be there and she would entertain them with stories from the Rectory, where she worked. She told them about the old clergyman and his wife. "He's a grand old man. But she's a tarter. No matter how much you do for her it's never enough."

She told them about his young nephew James and his beautiful fiancée, and would describe in detail her elegant clothes and fine jewellery. The Rectory and its inhabitants became very real to Eleanor and she waited patiently for each new piece of information about their lives.

One evening when Eleanor called, she found Molly crying by the kitchen fire.

"Old Reverend Thompson died," Mary explained, "The place has been left to his nephew, James." Then leaning closer to Eleanor, she said in a near whisper, "He left Molly a hundred pounds. Aye, he was a good man. Molly is giving the money to me. She's a good girl. Worth-a-rearing. And it seems the wife is going to live with a sister. At least that's a blessing. For she's a right divil. Aye, a right divil. And talking about divils, I heard another slanging match coming from your yard this morning again. I just wish she would come to some sort of agreement with Manny. It's not fair to you, nor to herself. And there was me thinking her trouble was over when he went. Aye, I wish she would give up and spend more time thinking about you, instead of having you slaving away for nothing. Aye, poor wee pet, this should be the best time of your life."

The hours spent with Mary, Molly and her grandfather made the turmoil of her early years bearable and she had never forgotten their kindness.

Eleanor was fifteen when her grandfather died. The memory of his passing was still painful all these years later, for she had grown to love and trust him. A few weeks after his death, she discovered that he had left her the house and it's contents and a sum of money when she reached eighteen. The joy and gratitude that she felt sent her flagging spirits soaring as she contemplated the future. She was determined to become a teacher and was showing 'good promise' as her teacher often told her. John Henderson had made provision for her education, setting up a bank account in her name and had given her the start in life that she could not have dreamed of just a few short years earlier. She wandered from room to room around the house, each room, each book, each ornament bringing happy, haunting memories of her grandfather.

Her mother was the only person that she had left of her own, and her continued unhappiness and obsession with keeping the farm brought gloom to her heart.

As she grew up, the situation at home remained static and hostile as endless battles for ownership of the farm continued relentlessly.

Eleanor finally left the farm at the age of nineteen and went to live in the home that her grandfather had provided for her at Creega Port. She had just returned home from her first day's teaching at Ballyneely school to find her mother once more locked in battle with Manny.

Later, when she had endured another detailed account of the day's battle Eleanor said, "Listen Mother. I've had enough. I can take no more of this hate … this constant fighting. I'm going to my own house at Crag and I'm offering you a home with me."

She fell silent, "What? Me leave what is rightfully mine to him? Just walk away and leave the farm to that upstart? You must be out of your mind if you think I'd just walk away now. No, I'll fight to the bitter end for what's mine."

Looking at her mother across the table, Eleanor noted how prematurely youth had left her face and decided to try again.

"Mother please, come with me. You can be your own boss in the house. I won't interfere and we'll have enough to live on."

"Have you not listened to what I said? I'm never walking out on what's rightfully mine. He's not getting my farm … and if you walk out on me, then so be it." Eleanor felt anger rising up inside her, until it finally exploded. Standing up she shouted,

"Walk out on you? I hate this place. I hate everything it stands for. Every memory I have is filled with fear and loneliness … and hard bloody work."

Standing up and moving closer to Eleanor, the anger blazing in her eyes, she shouted back, "After all I've done for you. I sacrificed everything for you. I came here against my better judgement for you. And now … you just walk away when I'm fighting for justice."

"You came here for me. That's a new line on it. I didn't ask to be born. You weren't raped. I don't know how you can blame me. My young life was ruined in this house with that brute of a man you married and you're not much better. And I'm supposed to be grateful, am I? My God, I don't believe what I'm hearing. You want me to stay here and help you fight for the rest of my days. Well, I'm not. I have a place of my own where I'm going to try to be at least content … though God only knows how I could live a normal life after everything I've been through. Do you know … I'm terrified of men? Every time I see a man, I think of him, with his big brutal fists. And now I'm supposed to stay and watch you fight with Manny for the rest of your days. And I thought that today would be different and that you'd greet me and ask about my first day's teaching at Ballyneely. You really are obsessed with this damned place. Well, I hate it … not one happy memory does it hold for me. So I'm going alone. If you want to stay and fight on for the rest of your days - then so be it."

As she packed her clothing, her anger was replaced by sadness; sadness for her mother, herself and all that might have been. She looked around the room that she had occupied for the last eighteen years and could only remember fear. The horrible sound of shouts and blows coming from the kitchen still resounded in her ears. "I must go, I must," she repeated to herself, afraid that the guilt at leaving her mother would take hold and stop her.

In the kitchen, she found her mother still sitting in the same position. They looked at each other in silence for a while as Eleanor's resolve to leave was beginning to wain. Her mother's blue eyes wore an expression of anxiety, and there were deep, tired lines on her face. Trouble had drained what was left of what must once have been a decided beauty and her features had a pinched look.
"Please come with me," Eleanor began, all the anger gone out of her. "Please. I'll look after you now and

you'll have a new life."

As Jane McGrath looked at her daughter she was struck again by the resemblance to James Henderson, the same brown eyes and curling auburn hair; the chin, the nose, they were all a mirror image of his features. Her eyes, seeking Eleanor's, had an unfathomable expression, a mixture of grief, longing and regret.

"Thank you for offering me a home with you. But I can't go. I can't leave it all to him. I've suffered too much. Here is where I belong and here I'll stay. Now you go and be happy. But before you go - tell me about today."

"It went well. Wee Mary Kate Quinn is one of my pupils. She's a lovely wee soul and very bright. But I overheard the others making comments about her background and I know how that hurts. I remember it well," she ended, with a sigh. Jane transferred her gaze from her daughter's face to the window and the fields beyond, the fields that she just couldn't let go. When she spoke again, her voice sounded distant, "I'm sorry for all the hurt. It would have been so different if he'd lived. As it is, I paid a heavy price for falling for him. I'm glad that you can help wee Mary Kate at school."

"So you won't come with me."

"No, I'm staying put."

"I'll be back to see you when I get settled in. And if you change your mind I'll be waiting."

"I won't."

When finally she left and walked through the dusk hung with the cold wet smell of rain, she could feel the tears that tangled in her thick eyelashes roll down her cheeks as her emotions ebbed and flowed between guilt and longing for a life of her own. Thoughts of Mary Kate came back to her, as she stumbled down the rough surface of the lane. "Mary Kate, has something I never knew - she has a loving family," she reminded herself. Then she reminded herself that she, at least, didn't have a rapist as a father.

Later at the door of the house, she stood back and whispered, "Home, my home". And as she walked inside, the feeling of having at last come home lightened her steps and she could feel a song in her heart. "Thank you - grandfather. Thank you," she whispered, to the empty hallway.

When she dismissed her class, to cheers of delight from her pupils, the long summer break left Eleanor feeling at a loose end. She had planned to do some work to the house, and then there was her mother. She gave a long low sigh at the thought of her. She would be in the kitchen looking worn and pale, but otherwise the scene was the same - the fire in the hearth, the darkening advance of a gloomy day and the sound of rain. Then she would begin another long, sorry tale of Manny's misdeeds to which Eleanor had to listen without interruption and only the thought of going home, having fulfilled her duty could lift her spirits.

On a warm June afternoon Eleanor was weeding the front garden when a stranger's voice interrupted her, she looked up to see an elderly woman staring at her. "My name's Jenny Magee. I bought your grandfather's old house and I'm here for a holiday. Your late grandfather was my third cousin. He lived beside us in Belfast. Anyhow, he wrote to me not long before he died and asked me to come and see you from time to time." Her next words sent Eleanor's thoughts reeling. "You are so like your father."

"How ... how do you know?" Eleanor stammered.

"I knew him from he was a baby. And I still cry at times when I think about his young life being cut so short. You would have been very proud of him."

Eleanor stared open mouthed at this strange, shrunken old woman who seemed to know her life story. "Where's my manners? Please come in," Eleanor urged, going towards the door.

During the following week Jenny Magee visited Eleanor daily, filling in all the missing gaps about her father. Two weeks later, Jenny asked her to come back with her to Belfast for a couple of weeks, "The change will do you good and there are people I'd like you to meet."

"Oh, I don't know. It's good of you to ask. But there's my mother to think about. I usually call once a day ... I'd feel guilty you see if I didn't."

Secrets on the Breeze

"By what you've told me, she is her own worst enemy and you have nothing to feel guilty about. She'll probably go into her box fighting for the farm and there is nothing you can do to stop her."

"You're probably right. But she is my mother and she suffered because of me."

"Poppycock Eleanor. She wasn't forced to become pregnant and you didn't ask for things to turn out the way they did. You are only young once and you nccd to live your young life to the full - make up for your miserable childhood."

"I'll think about it. Mind you I would like to see where he lived and see Belfast."

"Good. Get packed then and come," she said, her wrinkled face puckered into deep folds as she smiled.

"Right then, I'll go."

As she walked along the familiar laneways to tell her mother about her visit, she felt a little deflated. At the top of the hill she stood silently gazing around her. Budding heather and golden whins, the long sweep of the brown hills, and the deep plunge of the valley, the strong, salty smell of the shore was all about her, and she could see the swift silver of the sea below her. Suddenly, the beauty of her homeland stirred her very soul in a way she had never felt before and she walked on with a new determination.

Manny met her at the gateway, "That woman will be the death of me yet. This land is mine now and she won't get that through her thick head," he stormed, his face bright red with rage.

Eleanor sighed before she spoke, "It's not doing her any good either. I just wish you would try to come to some sort of agreement with her."

"What agreement? The farm was left to me because he didn't want her to have it. That's the truth of it. He done enough for her by marrying her in that condition in the first place."

Suddenly, Eleanor was consumed with anger. "He married her for three hundred pounds and a free servant into the bargain. She has had more bruises than you've had dinners. It was a life of hell on earth - and I know because I was there. He was an evil scum of a man that I'm thankful to have no blood ties with. If it was me, I'd be out of here, for they'll be no luck with it. But my mother rightly feels that she earned the oul' farm with her own blood, sweat and tears."

"He reared you and you would have been brought up a bastard only for him."

Eleanor's whole body shook with anger. With as much control as she could manage she took two steps closer to where he stood. Then looking into his eyes she said in low controlled tones, "Wouldn't I have been the lucky one to have been brought up a bastard? Instead I had to endure a life of hell under his roof. An unpaid slave - living in a hellhole. That's the way he treated a defenceless, innocent child. You are welcome to his farm as far as I'm concerned.

But I'll defend my mother with my last ounce of strength." She stared at him in silence for a few seconds before she said, "Stay away from my mother if you know what's good for you."

"I'll win on the day of the court case - you'll see if I won't."

"I can't wait. Won't I have a story to tell?" she added, with a smile of contempt.

His face blazing, he stared at her for a few moments before walking away.

When he had disappeared from sight, she sunk down onto the low wall exhausted and shaking.

"Good for you Eleanor," her mother's voice made her jump. "And there was me thinking you had no spunk in you."

"I didn't want to get involved with this. He just made my blood boil. But I still think you should leave this miserable hole and let him do what he likes with it. And in spite of what I said, I would hate to get up on a witness stand and air all my past. I'd hate it," she repeated, getting to her feet.

"It won't come to that. He won't give in. But he hasn't the nerve for a court battle either. I've been doing some jobs to the house. Young Johnny has been helping me. He finished his term down below and I hired him for six months.

He's a grand lad and a great worker. Come and see all the jobs we done," she said, with a cheerfulness that Eleanor had never witnessed before. As they walked towards the front of the house, Eleanor told her about her forthcoming visit to Belfast. "The break will do you good," was all she said, leaving Eleanor feeling both puzzled and relieved.

In spite of the whitewash, the newly gleaming paintwork, the closely-clipped hedges and wedded paths, to Eleanor's mind it would always be a house of darkness and suffering and disillusioned old age, and she hoped never to sleep under its roof again.

Belfast opened up a new horizon to Eleanor and she felt at home in Jenny's big house in a leafy, affluent area in the east of the city. She met Peter Mullins, a tall young man of twenty-two, with grey-green eyes and a smile that left her weak at the knees and during the coming days, he was to walk with her, waltz with her and kiss her passionately at every opportunity and they were destined to fall deeply in love. Looking back, she knew she had fallen in love at first sight.

During her two weeks in Belfast, Peter made each day count as he showed her around the city. They climbed Divis Mountain and looked at the grandeur of the castle on their way back. They walked through the mean streets as the mill workers made their way home after a hard days labour as Peter told her about the sectarian conflicts of a divided community. "That's why I'm going to America" he had said. At these words, Eleanor could feel a lump come into her throat as she struggled to smile. "I have an uncle in shipping and he has offered me a job - a good job. I was on the furniture design team for the new ship that's being built here, it's called '*Titanic*'. We'll go and see her tomorrow. Anyhow, my uncle Joe has offered me a similar job in Boston."

It was later that evening that they kissed for the first time and the memory of that kiss lived with her for the rest of her life. During the coming months, out of the ashes of that first love, something much greater had risen, like a new day's sun over the sea.

By the end of the two weeks, Peter told her he loved her and asked her to go to America with him. She had felt the warm heaviness of joy and longing spread from her heart through her whole body. It was finally agreed that she would join him in Boston when he had found them a place to live. "I will write every day until we can be together forever," he had told her on the night before her departure.

Eleanor looked across at Sara with tears glistening in her eyes. "He came here to Donegal to see me before he boarded the *Titanic* at Queenstown on April 10th 1912. It's still painful to remember for he was the only real love of my life.

But, life had to go on and I devoted myself to my teaching and supporting my mother in her lifetime battle with Manny for the farm. She finally came to live with me during the war. She outlived Manny by five years and sold the farm to a local man." Then shaking her head, she smiled at Sara, "She was a stubborn one. Aye, stubborn as a mule. But I wish she had showed me the love and courage that you gave your daughter and Mary Kate."

The two women sat silently in the twilight for a while before Sara spoke, "I didn't know you had suffered so much Eleanor. As for the early years - I know only too well the price of keeping secrets like that. I often wondered over the years why a beautiful woman like you hadn't married - now I think I know why."

Eleanor gazed at the smouldering fire before she spoke again, "There have been other men since, but none that could take his place. He was the only one that I told my story to, until now. You see, I had a very low opinion of myself back then and I was sure that he'd reject me. But I was wrong. Don't be sad for me - for I've come to a contented middle-age in spite of everything. And do you know Sara, I wonder if I would have been really happy in America? Leaving my mother and the house that my grandfather left me. I'd have missed the place in spite of myself."

"The first time I set eyes on you was on Mary Kate's first day at school. And I thought you were the most beautiful looking young woman I'd ever set eyes on. Little did I know then, how much sorrow lay behind your smile," Sara ended in a sigh.

When she had gone Sara sat in the semi-darkness contemplating all that Eleanor had told her and felt sorrow at how much of her young life had been lived in the grip of fear, seeing its shadows darken her existence.

She was roused from her deep thought by the sound of James's voice coming from the kitchen and suddenly she felt excited about telling him of the strong possibility of Mary Kate getting the teaching post at Clougher.

Chapter 5

Sara's Journey

It was not on the surface of things a time for gloom, as Sara watched the yellow daffodils on the hillsides swaying in the spring sun. As the train curled its way around the hillsides nearing Clougher station, her feelings of unease increased. The letter from her old friend and former neighbour Grace Murphy left her with feelings of foreboding. The train plunged into a tunnel, dusky dark, and roaring with echoes. Sara sat huddled in her woollen coat. She let the letter flutter to the floor.

Why she couldn't have told her in the letter what was on her mind rather than drag her all this way mystified her. Grace had the same secret that she couldn't share with her husband that Sara had. Grace's daughter, Eleanor, had also been the victim of Seamus Quinn's evil. As she neared her destination Sara became more anxious, "Let it have nothing to do with him," she whispered to herself.

The train stopped at a siding, just before the station. From the window Sara could just make out her old home tucked under Clougher hill. She could vividly remember when she first saw the cottage that was to be her future home all those years ago. John Quinn had pointed it out to her from this very spot. It hurt her now to remember all the hopes and dreams she had back then. But she reminded herself that the past few years had been contented years and apart from childhood, the happiest years in her entire life.

When James Thompson had stopped drinking, and had come to terms with his wife's death, life began to change for the better in every way.

She remembered how she had been the subject of local gossip and ridicule.

To leave a husband, and seek shelter under another man's roof in 1920s rural Ireland was almost a crime, no matter what the circumstances.

Then in her head she could hear James Thompson's quiet dependable voice saying, "You have always been true to yourself Sara. They don't matter." Then she would straighten her back, hold her head high and walk on. James Thompson was without a doubt her best friend. He had given her refuge all those years ago when she had rescued her granddaughter from the fate of the orphanage. Now that refuge had become home, a home where she felt safe and secure. What a contrast from the evening of her first arrival, when she cradled Mary Kate in her arms. She could smell the damp of neglect and feel the hopelessness of its two inhabitants. And into this, she brought a small, helpless baby. Now that tiny baby was a happy, confident and beautiful young woman who filled their lives with joy. But yet, Sara had this overpowering need to protect her from the brutal truth of her beginnings.

 The train screeched forward towards the station and Sara was confronted again with matters of the present.

She walked swiftly through the village and on up the lane towards Cougher hill. Grace met her at door with a smile, but behind the smile her eyes spoke of trouble. Her husband sat at the table. "Well Sara, you're a stranger," he said, with a look of surprise that told her he was not aware of the letter.

Gulping the last of the tea from his mug, he got up from the table. "I must get on. Work to be done." he said as he went.

Grace busied herself clearing the table, and putting on the kettle before she spoke. Then turning around to face Sara, she said, "I'm that glad you've come.

Secrets on the Breeze

I'm beside myself with fear, and I can't confide in anyone else." Sara could feel her stomach churn with apprehension as she waited for Grace to tell her what was wrong.

Sitting down heavily in the chair she said, "It's him. It's the old house. They are re-roofing it."

"Who? What house?"

"Seamus Quinn's. They say he's coming back." She felt a sudden lump in her throat, and an old dread return to the pit of her stomach. "Oh, dear God no. Not this," she almost screamed. She remembered all the nights she had dreamed about him over the last twenty years and woke oppressed by fear. Then she would leave her bed and walk over to the window. Outside there might be moonlight, or fresh snow, or wind driven leaves, or a soft spring night like the coming night might be. And she would stare into the shadows until the fear of his evil would disappear with the first flush of dawn.

Looking across at Grace she asked, "Are you sure? I thought ... no, hoped he was dead."

"I know. And, how … oh how I wish I was wrong Sara."

"We will think of something Grace. We must stop him. I'll talk to James. He'll know what to do," she added, with more confidence than she felt.

"Many a time I was tempted to tell Danny. But I know it would have caused more trouble. He would have found him and killed him long ago. And anyway,

Ellen doesn't want her father to know."
"Thanks for warning me Grace. And try not to worry too much."

Sara's mind was filled with troubled thoughts on the train ride home. She hated having to give him bad news, which was sure to disturb his present peace of mind. They had been delighted at the thought of Mary Kate coming home to teach in Clougher, thanks to Eleanor Donnelly's intervention.

He appeared in the hallway just as she was hanging her coat. "I'll get you some tea. I've made some soup. I suppose you would call it a sort of stew" he said, with a lopsided grin. "Oh, well done."

"Don't praise me yet 'till you've tasted it. As you know, cooking is not my strong point."

Sitting down at the table she tasted the soup. "Mme, it tastes good," she said with a smile.

When she finished the soup, he said. "Come on into the drawing-room. There is a good fire." As she stood up to clear the table, he caught her arm. "Leave the dishes. Come and tell me what the summons to Clougher was all about." Seated at either side of the fire, his glance was direct and pleasant. "Well are you going to tell me?" As she told him about the day's events she could see his face darken. They both sat in silence for a while staring at the flames of the fire. "I knew something was wrong from the minute you came through the door. I thought we were safe from bellowing breakers like this, after all this time," his voice trailed away in a sigh.

"So did I, James. So did I."

"Somehow we must prevent this man coming back into our midst. The law should have dealt with the likes of him long ago. But, as that's not possible, we must deal with it ourselves"

"How?" "She asked quietly. Then before he had time to answer, she went on, "I shouldn't involve you. You have done enough."

"If I were doing good deeds for you - for the rest of my days, Sara, I would never have done enough." Reaching across the space between them, he took her hand. "Don't look so tragic. It will be all right, somehow."

She smiled at him in gratitude, and knew that she loved him, not in a romantic sense, but with a deep respect for the friendship and loyalty that had grown over all the years that she had known him. As she looked at his quiet countenance she felt comforted.

"I couldn't bear Mary Kate to know that he is her father; that her mother was raped by that evil man," Sara said quietly.

"She won't have to know. I'll make discreet inquiries tomorrow and if I can find his whereabouts ... we'll put the fear of God in him. Threaten him with what John failed to finish."

Sara smiled across at him and as he returned her smile,

she felt comforted.

Chapter 6

Canada 1945

Jean McGreggor crunched her way across the snow-covered street deep in her own thoughts. She felt happier than she had done since she arrived in this cold wilderness. Just this evening Jim had agreed to go back to Toronto in time for the birth of their new baby. As she picked her way towards the post office with the letter in her pocket that would convey the good news to her mother, she almost tripped over him. As she struggled to regain her balance, she heard a groan coming from the hump on the ground at her feet. Bending down she made out the form of a man lying face down in the snow. Gasping, she struggled and managed to turn him over. In the eerie moonlight she could see his face was swollen and bruised, his clothes caked with frozen snow. She lifted his head a little and immediately felt warm sticky blood on her hand. He was breathing in harsh, pain-racked gasps and muttering, but she couldn't make out anything he was saying. "I'll get help. Don't worry," she added as she half ran towards the yellow glow of light in the distance. A young man answered her urgent knocking. "There's a man lying badly injured along the street. He needs help badly." Grabbing a coat, he called inside. "Harry, get the truck."

Ten minutes later she sat cradling his head in the back of the truck as they slowly made their way through rough snow-covered roads towards Mercy Hospital.

When they pulled up at the emergency door, the driver ran inside and returned with a porter and a young nurse. "Who is he? What happened?" she asked, feeling his wrist for a pulse.

"I don't know. I found him lying on the road, and with the help of these two men brought him here."

Inside the hospital she sat down on a chair along a grey corridor to wait. Later the two young strangers came over to join her. "Will we be needed for anything? We would need to be getting back."

"You go. I'll wait and see if he is going to make it. And thanks," she added.

Ten minutes later a middle-aged doctor appeared

along the corridor and stopped beside her. "I'm Doctor Bond." Are you the lady that found the injured man?" She nodded.

"But I don't know who he is, or what happened to him. Is he still alive?"

"Yes, but he is badly injured. His head injuries are the biggest worry."

"I need to go home. I didn't get time to tell my husband where I'd be," Jean said

"Oh, of course. Do you have transport?" She shook her head. "In that case we can arrange something for you - and if you find out anything about his identity, let us know."

"I will. I hope he makes it." He smiled down at her momentarily, and was gone.

Unable to put this stranger that she had stumbled upon out of her mind she returned the following afternoon to enquire if he was still alive. On arrival she was recognized by the same nurse, who came over to greet her. "He has regained consciousness. But he can't remember what happened to him," she added. And it seems he has no relatives. Would you like to see him? Being as he almost certainly owes his life to you."

The nurse led her over to his bedside. His head was heavily bandaged and his eyes remained closed while she observed him in silence. Clearing her throat she asked, "How are you feeling today?" He opened his eyes and stared at her, a stare that made her feel uncomfortable.

"You're not from the police?" She shook her head. "I'm Jean Mc Greggor. I found you the other night." A look of fear and suspicion came into his eyes, before he asked, "Did you see or hear anything?"

"No. I almost fell over you lying on the road." She watched the suspicious fear leave his eyes and again felt discomforted by his stare. "I don't know what happened. I was struck from behind. Damned police keep asking me the same questions over and over," he said averting his eyes away from her. As she walked down the hospital corridor she heard someone calling her name. "Ah, Mrs McGreggor, I'm glad I caught you," the same doctor that she saw on the first night said, as he hastily made his way towards her.

"While he was still unconscious, the nurse found a letter in his pocket. Seems his name is Seamus Quinn from a place called Clougher, Donegal, Ireland. He's a long way from home. I've written a letter to that address. It will take ages to get a reply though. Says he doesn't remember his name. Not uncommon after head injuries. Did you manage to find out anything?" She shook her head.

"Pity. He's nearly ready to go home. That's if he has a home to go to," he added.

"I suppose, I could give him a room at my place in the meantime," Jean said, a little hesitantly, suddenly remembering her husband and how he might react to her generosity. "That's if my husband agrees."

"We must learn more about him if we are to solve our mystery," Doctor Bond added. "Anyway, if your husband agrees to his staying with you for a time … well so much the better. Personally, I believe he's been beaten up by somebody."

"He seemed scared to me. Bothered about the police questioning him."

"It certainly is a mystery. Thanks anyway for all your help Mrs McGreggor."

When supper was over Jean looked across at David, "That man that I found unconscious - well, he has regained consciousness. Did you find out anything about him?"

"I asked a few people at the mine. They seemed to know very little. But I got a hunch that they know more than they're letting on."

"Why do you think that," Jean asked, eagerly.

"Well, when I was talking about it yesterday, two of the men gave a sort of anxious glance at each other. But they're saying nothing."

"That figures. Dr. Bond thinks he was beaten up."

"Well, if he was beaten up by one, or the two that I'm thinking of, he deserved it."

"Why do you say that?" Jean responded.

"Because they're not violent men. Decent men - both of them. And I was just wondering myself - why a man of his age would come to a wilderness like this.

Mining is a young man's pursuit. He must be in his fifties at least."

"David, would you mind if I offered him a room for a few days? Just 'till he gets back on his feet."

"Now, Jean. I don't think that's a wise thing to do. He could be a murderer for all we know."

"I know, I know. But, hc's a stranger in this frozen land with nobody of his own. I just feel sorry for him, that's all."

"You let your heart rule your head too much Jean. Look, let me see if I can find out anymore about him first. You have a kind heart and I suppose that's why I fell in love with you," he ended, as a soft indulgent smile crossed his face.

In the morning, Jean watched as a long, pale beam of sunlight slanted through the east window. Not since October had the sun's arc risen high enough to send morning light through that window. Jean's hopes were high as she contemplated the arrival of their child and the reunion with her family at home.

Suddenly, thoughts of the stranger in the hospital returned to trouble her. She now wished that she hadn't offered him lodgings. What if David was right and he was dangerous? And yet, she felt that she owed him a chance to recover from whatever misfortune had befallen him.

She filled the stove with logs before getting her coat, fur hat and scarf.

Secrets on the Breeze

Outside a fresh snow had fallen and the air was crisp and cold.

Standing by the clump of pine trees, where the bus usually ran she saw Helen Southerland coming towards her. Helen lived on the next block and was a constant source of comfort to Jean. In her lonely days she often confided in her and they shared their longings to return home. "Do you know if there's a bus due?" she asked, as Helen's figure moved closer. "It should be due anytime. I'm going up to Mercy Hospital. Where are you heading?" Helen enquired. "I'm off up to the hospital too. I'm going to enquire after the man I found near death the other evening." Helen looked troubled and uncomfortable as she looked at Jean. "I would have nothing more to do with him if I were you," she finally ventured.
"Why?"
"I'm not at liberty to say. But please just have no more to do with him."
Looking at Helen, Jean wondered why she even bothered to consult her.
Was it the lack of female company that had caused a friendship between them in the first place? she pondered as they boarded the bus.
Before they reached the hospital, Jean had decided to ignore the older woman's advice and do what she thought best for the stranger.
Jean had a stubborn streak that hated to be put down.

Although she recognised the dangers that this stranger might bring, she was determined to do what she thought best. Keeping the home fires burning, cooking and cleaning had left her unfulfilled as a human being, and when a chance to do something worthwhile presented itself, she was determined to seize it.

She found Seamus Quinn seated in a chair by the bedside when she went into the ward. "Glad to see you sitting up. How are you feeling?" she enquired. "Better. But before you ask, I remember nothing. Don't even know who I am," he answered, barely glancing at her.

The speedy way he volunteered this information and the unease in his whole demeanour, told Jean he was hiding something.

"Your name is Seamus. Seamus Quinn, from Ireland."

"Who told you that?" he asked, with apprehension in his tone.

"While you were unconscious, the nurse found a letter in your pocket addressed to Seamus Quinn."

A look of near terror came into his eyes, "Who was the letter from? I want it back now."

"Don't worry. The nurse has kept it safely for you."

"Go and tell her I want it now," he said, his face blazing.

"No need to get annoyed like that, it'll not help your recovery. We are only trying to help you."

"Please go and get the letter." His tone had changed, his voice pleading, but she noted his eyes still held a look of fear.

"All right I'll see what I can do."

She found the same nurse seated at a desk in a small office. "It's Seamus Quinn," she began, "he wants the letter you found. He seems almost desperate."

"Oh, the police have it. Seems they are writing to their counterparts in Ireland to see if we can identify him."

"He'll not be pleased," Jean sighed. "He seems very agitated."

"Do you want me to explain it to him?"

"Would you?"

Jean followed the nurse back to his bedside. "The police have borrowed your letter Mr Quinn. They are trying to find out if you have any relatives."

A look of terror came into his eyes and his voice came in a hoarse whisper, "They had no right - no right. It's my property and you shouldn't have give it to them."

"We are only trying to help you. You have no need to get yourself all worked up like this."

"Either you get it back for me right now or I'm leaving, memory or no memory," he shouted.

"It's only a letter and the police are trying to help you just like we are. All this agitation is doing you no good," the nurse said, trying to pacify him in whatever way she could.

Turning his fearful gaze to Jean, he asked, "Will you go?"

His face was ashen, and the eyes that met hers were fearful and pleading, it stirred in her both unease and pity.

"I'll try. But I very much doubt that they will be willing to give the letter to me."

"Just try - please," he added, grasping her hand tightly.

It took almost an hour to reach the police station and Jean had to confess that she enjoyed the walk, feeling the first hint of warmth from the sun and a feeling of oneness under the immense sky.

She sighed before reaching the door of the police office, her earlier feeling of well-being vanished.

"Can I help you?" a young man's voice asked from behind the small desk.

"I'm Jean McGreggor. I found an injured man named Quinn about ten days ago, lying in the snow. Anyhow, he's recovering at the hospital and wants the letter the nurses gave you. Thinks it might jog his memory. He has lost his memory."

"Better see Mac about that. Follow me."

"Mac" was a middle-aged man with bright blue, searching eyes that peered out at her from under red-brown bushy eyebrows.

When she had repeated her request, he gave her a long searching look before he spoke.

"How much do you know about this man?" he asked, his quizzical stare making her feel uncomfortable.

Secrets on the Breeze

"I know little or nothing about him."

"Why are you going to the bother of ... all this?" he asked, lifting his hands palms upwards towards her.

A feeling of annoyance crept over her, and in a slightly raised voice she said, "He's a stranger who's a long way from home. He's lost his memory and has no one of his own. He thought - that is we both thought, that reading the letter might jog his memory. It is his letter after all," she ended.

"It is his letter and he can have it back. It tells us nothing anyway, just something about house repairs and a new roof. But, I have a hunch that he knows more that he's letting on. I believe he'd been beaten up and it wasn't for his good deeds. I have no proof mind you, just a strong hunch. So, I'd be careful if I were you."

"Anyway, the rules say that I must deliver the letter myself. I can do it now. Can give you a lift there if you like."

She hesitated for a moment, then decided to accept his offer.

They remained silent on the five-minute journey, each lost in their own thoughts. Mac parked close to the hospital entrance and reached into the back seat for a folder.

"Could I have a look at the letter for a minute?" she asked. He handed it to her in silence. When she had read it she fumbled in her bag for a pencil and notebook, then wrote down the address of the sender.

Mac sat straight, looking intently at her with one eyebrow raised in gesture.

"Might I enquire why?"

"I thought it might be an idea to write to the place mentioned in the letter - there might be some relatives - some answers."

He sighed and stared straight ahead as if trying to reach a decision.

"Look," he began "I believe this man has done something to one of the miners' children. I'm not sure. They won't talk - just hints and innuendos, nothing that we can charge him with. So this is strictly between me and you."

Jean nodded her agreement.

"If you want to write to that address, then OK. But nothing of this, it's only local gossip I'm going on and that counts for nowt in law."

There was silence for a moment and then he asked, "One more thing. Don't let him know you suspect anything for now. I'm following one more line of enquiry in New York. We found details of a bank account on a scrap of rumpled paper from his pocket. If he suspects anything he'd do a runner - memory loss or not."

"I'll try and act as normal as possible," Jean replied, as flutters of fear and excitement took hold of her.

"Don't forget - don't breathe a word," he warned, as they went through the main entrance.

They found him sitting in an armchair by the bedside

and when he looked up and saw them coming towards him, a look of panic crept into his eyes.

"Jean says you want your letter back. Rules say I must deliver it in person.

Hope it helps to retrieve some memory for you." He held out his hand, "Goodbye Mr Quinn and good luck with your recovery." They shook hands and Mac nodded briefly at Jean before he walked away.

Trying to sound as casual as possible, Jean said, "I will leave you now to read your letter in peace. I must get back and cook the evening meal or I'll be in trouble."

"Before you go - what did they say when you asked for the letter?"

"Oh, nothing much. Just said it was no use to them anyway."

She watched his face muscles relax and knew that she had succeeded in her efforts not to arouse his suspicions.

At home she prepared the dinner and sat down to write the letter to Donegal, Ireland.

Chapter 7

The Road For Home

Mary Kate awoke from a heavy sleep. And as she looked around her, the realisation that she was at home again in her own room sent shivers of delight through her. Every corner of the room was familiar to her, every item, from the cracks in the ceiling to the pattern on the curtains brought happy contentment. She remembered telling her friend Mary in Dublin about her room and its history, and about it being the room that was once occupied by James Thompson and his new bride.

"She died in the room you sleep in," she had exclaimed, in horror.

"Well, if her ghost is still around - then it's a happy ghost," Mary Kate had told her.

She thought again about her interview of the day before and she dared to hope that she would be offered the job. Her grandmother had told her about Eleanor Donnelly's recommendation of her and she decided to visit Eleanor to thank her before she returned to Dublin.

Suddenly bounding out of bed she went to the window and pulled back the curtains. Her gaze moved from the rocks far below to the vast expanse of shimmering ocean and the golden gorse rolling its golden tide across the hillside. Opening the window wide, she listened to the song of the cuckoo, as she breathed deeply of the pure, scented air, her attention was drawn to the figure working in the grey-walled garden below her window. As she watched his bent frame, her eyes misted over and her heart was warm with joy. As she watched, he straightened his back, resting on the handle of the spade. He looked up and saw her as a smile lit up his kindly, craggy face, "Good morning," he called.

"Good morning father," she called back, "I'll be down in a few minutes."

She remembered the time, in this very room, when she had asked him if he was her father and the answer he had given her. "I'm not your biological father Mary Kate - I wish I were. But I feel like your father in every other sense," he had replied. Then she had asked him if she could call him father. He had smiled in the way she had just witnessed and said, "Nothing would give me greater pleasure." Why she could not be satisfied and give up the quest for finding her real father, she could not fathom. But she could not rid herself of this need to know.

The appetising smell of frying bacon scented the hallway and she rushed towards the kitchen. "Good morning love. Sleep well?"

"Like a log. The smell of the bacon reminds me that I'm starving. The landlady in Dublin could have done with a few lessons from you. Greasy bacon and cabbage night after night."

"I have Molly to thank for my cooking skills."

"I was just thinking about Molly before I got up. She was so good to me when I was wee. I used to stand on a chair here at the table and watch her prepare the food. She always gave me a mixture to stir or a bowl to lick."

Sara sighed deeply and when she looked again at Mary Kate, her eyes had misted over. "Poor Molly. May God rest her and I hope she's happy. For she was a good friend to us."

"I'm going over to see Eleanor Donnelly later to thank her for recommending me," Mary Kate said, changing the subject.

"Good. She's a lovely woman is Eleanor. And God knows she didn't have her sorrows to seek either."

"Oh. I always thought that Eleanor had a fairly easy

Secrets on the Breeze

life. She lives in a lovely old house and has her teaching, which she always seemed to love."

"Aye, I know that on the surface of things it looks that way. But she has known her troubles too. She told me her life story one time. She might tell you her story one day too. I don't want to break her confidence."

As Mary Kate watched Sara, she detected unease about her and she had a feeling that something was bothering her.

She decided not to quiz her about it for now and left for Eleanor's after breakfast.

The shore road twisted and turned under the craggy, rocky hills and soon the sun broke through the high cloud. As she neared Eleanor's house Mary Kate found a flat spot and lay down on her stomach gazing out to sea. Somewhere a church bell was ringing, ding-dong, ding-dong, echoed in the still air. A man in a white short-sleeved shirt ambled along the sandy path leading from the beach. As he drew level, he smiled down at her, "Lovely morning," he said.

His voice was warm and friendly and as she looked up and met his gaze she observed the deepest, blue eyes she had ever seen.

Scrambling to her feet, she dusted herself down and slipped her feet back into her shoes.

"I'm Mike Reid," he said, holding out his hand.

"Mary Kate Quinn. Nice to meet you, Mike."

"I'm here to visit a friend, Eleanor Donnelly," he

began, "But she already has a visitor, and I decided to take a walk while I'm waiting."

Mary Kate smiled, "That is where I'm heading; to visit Eleanor."

"What a small world. We might as well sit down for a while and admire the view then," he said, sitting down on the coarse grass at her feet. Mary Kate sat down, a little self-consciously beside him. They sat in silence for a while before he asked, "Are you related to Eleanor?"

"No, just an old friend. She was once my teacher. Are you related?"

He shook his head, "Not exactly. I'm the nephew of her one-time fiancé. He went down with the Titanic in 1912. I first met her in Belfast when I was a wee lad - before my uncle left on the ill-fated ship. She says I look like him."

Mary Kate leaned both arms on her drawn up knees and gazed out to sea, and beyond towards Inistrahull Island, her thoughts on Eleanor's fiancé and his ill-fated journey.

She thought about Eleanor carrying the pain of having loved and lost. The man and the woman who had fallen in love, had imagined a world and a future between them - and had not lived to know what it might have been.

When she glanced across at Mike, his eyes were intently upon her and she could feel herself blush.

"I didn't know that Eleanor had lost someone like

that," she said with a sigh, her gaze shifting back to the far horizon.

"Do you live here all of the time?" he asked.

She shook her head. During the following thirty minutes she found herself telling him the story of her life. When she had finished there was only the sound of the sea lapping on the shore and the sighing wind in the reeds around their feet.

Mike sat motionless watching her for a long while and thought how beautiful she was, her dark curling hair, hazel eyes and a rapturous smile that sent his spirits soaring. And yet, he sensed moments of a solemn, tender, thoughtful and almost remorseful sadness.

"I'm willing to bet you're a great teacher," he remarked, breaking the poignant silence between them.

"I try to be. What do you do? For a living I mean."

"I'm a Marine Architect. Just recently qualified, so they don't let me loose on my own just yet. But it's interesting work. Wish I could live here though. Although I grew up in Belfast; I don't feel at home there. Too many tensions all the time. You know - the old sectarian thing."

"How did you get here to Donegal?"

"Like I said, I'm the nephew of Eleanor's late fiancé. We lived next door to a cousin of Eleanor's grandfather and they bought his old home. My family came here with them for holidays ever since."

Hazel McIntyre

They saw a cyclist peddling slowly towards them from the direction of Eleanor's house. "Here comes Eleanor's visitor. The coast will be clear now," Mike said, getting to his feet.

As he drew closer, Mary Kate recognised Father Connor. "Hallo Father Connor," she ventured as he came alongside, memories of the interview from the previous day at the forefront of her mind.

"Ah, Miss-Miss Quinn," he said, with a smile. "Now that you're here I would like a word with you." Walking a few paces from where they stood, he indicated for her to follow him. "Excuse us a minute," he said to Mike, as they walked a few paces away.

Mary Kate's emotions went from dread to hope, as she waited for him to speak.

"Thought I might as well tell you about our decision - on the teaching post.

We have decided to offer you the post. Not a word about it to anyone yet. We haven't got the letters out yet."

"Thank you - thank you."

"Well deserved." he answered, shaking her hand.

"I take it you've had good news, judging by the look on your face," Mike commented, when she rejoined him.

"Very good news. I've been offered the teaching job. No more Dublin grime and mean streets."

Smiling down at her, he suddenly stopped and kissed her lightly on the cheek, "Congratulations."

Secrets on the Breeze

She looked surprised and then she laughed. "This has been a strange day," she said, with a sigh of contentment, "Meeting you … getting the job, this place; just everything."

"It's been a day to remember for me too. How about I take you out to celebrate. To a dance or the pictures. Whatever you want."

"I'd like that. But I have to work out my notice in Dublin. Only two weeks 'till the school holidays."

"When you come back then."

"Right. You're on."

During the following days, Mary Kate's thoughts went back to Mike and that magical day. The memory of his kiss, however brief, seemed to leave its tracks, a permanent marking on her body and memory. It was there forever.

During class, he would suddenly come back into her mind: the slightly waved black hair; his athletic body, tall, slender and muscular; the quick smile that could turn to a surprising look of seriousness; his Irish-Scotch intensity and his friendly charm left their mark on her memory, as she counted the days until her homecoming.

Saying farewell to her class was far more painful than she had anticipated.

"Please don't leave us Miss," a small voice spoke from the doorway, as she was about to leave for the last time. Sally was one of the girls from the orphanage, and her sorrowful countenance brought tears to Mary Kate's eyes.

"Will I never, ever see you again?" she asked sorrowfully.

As she looked at her small, pinched face, Mary Kate wanted to gather her up in her arms and take her home. "We will write to each other Sally. And I'll ask the Mother General if I can take you up to Donegal for a holiday. But don't mention it yet. I will write and ask permission first."

Suddenly her small face lit up with joy. "Oh, thank you Miss."

Mary Kate gathered her up in her arms and rocked her gently, her tears mingling with her tangled hair as she silently vowed to keep her promise to her.

She gave a final glance around the familiar classroom and closed the door.

Outside, she bade a fond farewell to her colleagues and as she walked towards the gate she glimpsed Mary Reardon's face at a window, and could sense her spiteful gaze as her footsteps echoed on the cobbled path.

Chapter 8

The Letter

Sara gave a final satisfied glance around Mary
Kate's room before closing the door. Downstairs in
the drawing-room she set about making a fire. Once
it was blazing she swept the hearth. She stood for a
few minutes looking around the room with its familiar
objects and felt a sense of pride. Everything about
the old house gave Sara a sense of satisfaction and
security and her joy would be complete when Mary
Kate came home this very day.

From the hallway, she could hear the sound of voices
coming from the kitchen. "Ah, Sara. Jimmy here, has
a letter addressed to 'The Quinn Family' and

wondered if it might be for you. Sara examined the envelope carefully and couldn't recognise the handwriting or the Canadian postmark.

"You're the only Quinn the Post Office could come up with so you might as well open it," Jimmy said.

As she began opening the letter a feeling of foreboding came over her and as she read Jean McGreggor's account of Seamus Quinn's supposed memory loss, she froze. Suddenly remembering Jimmy she said, "Aye, it is for me. It's about a relation of John's."

She waited impatiently for Jimmy to leave, so she could scrutinise the letter further and talk it over with James.

When at last he went, she slumped down in the chair and handed the letter to him. He studied it in silence for a while before he spoke. "At least we know where he is now. It took three weeks for this letter to get here. Would there be a chance he's still there?"

"Probably scarpered by now," Sara replied.

"He might and he might not."

"Fancy this happening today of all days. I was so happy just a few minutes ago. Just finished getting Mary Kate's room ready," she ended in a sigh.

"We decide now what we are going to do about this letter. Do it - and put it right out of our heads. We spent too much of our precious time already worrying about that evil scum of a bastard."

Sara looked at him for a long while in silence and wondered all over again how she would manage if he weren't here and she had to face this alone. She could feel her body shudder at the thought. "Now Sara, don't go getting yourself all worked up about this business again. Nothing's worth that."

"Ah, no James. It's just that I was thinking what I'd do without you. And the mere thought of not having you to lean on ... sent shivers down my spine."

"Oh, Sara, Sara, haven't I told you enough times how I could never repay you - not if I lived ten life times. I often think about what I'd have done if you hadn't come to my rescue that night long ago. Probably in the grave years ago. Now I have you and Mary Kate and a comfortable home, good home-cooking and a true friend. Aye, that is the best bit."

They looked at each other in silence for a while before he spoke again, "I have something important to ask you Sara. But it can wait 'till we get this business out of the way," he said, glancing at the letter that he still held in his hand.

An hour later they had composed a letter to Jean McGreggor and a wire to the Newfoundland police, with just enough information to convey the fact, that John Quinn was a man to fear and that he would not be welcome in Ireland either. James decided to cycle to Clougher and hire a taxi to take him to a town ten miles away to send their correspondence, "It would be all over Clougher by nightfall if I sent it from there," he concluded.

When he had gone Sara began preparing the dinner, trying to take James's advice and not to let the episode spoil Mary Kate's homecoming. But, try as she might the feeling of sick-dread wouldn't go away.

Mary Kate's journey home was a journey of joy tinged with sadness at parting with the children and colleagues who had become her friends. Yet the joy of coming home far outweighed the grief of parting. The bus ride through familiar territory sent her spirits soaring high and the reunion with Sara and James lay at the end of the journey. Thoughts of Mike came and went. "Will I ever see him again?" she whispered. She secretly hoped that she would, for he had left a lasting impression on her mind. Then there was the new teaching post which with hindsight made her feel both apprehensive and excited. She was under no illusion about the narrow-mindedness of the rural community from which she came. The mean-spirited were sure to delve into her background and find it wanting. "Eleanor will know how I should handle things," she whispered to herself, making a decision to visit her at the earliest opportunity. She secretly smiled at the memory of her last visit to Eleanor's old house on the shore road. Mike's face came back into her mind again despite her best efforts not to hope. Her thoughts wandered back to her growing years and all that had gone before.

Those were difficult years for her too. Loved as she

was, cared for and watched over, still she had her lonely paths to tread, and still she had the unutterable fear of unspoken secrets as she groped in dark shadows, lighted only by a tiny torch of an instinct only half comprehended. She was changing, and not only she; the world she knew was changing. Ireland herself was changing; rousing from her long drugged sleep of complacency; waking reluctantly, fretfully to a new day.

James stood at the stop when the bus pulled in and he smiled broadly as she emerged down the steps. "Welcome home," he beamed. "You look well. A beautiful young woman," he said, with a slight shake of the head.

"We'll get the hackney car up. Too long a walk carrying bags.

Your grandmother is waiting for us - dinner at the ready."

"I can't wait to get there, I'm so happy to be home." The joyful smile that she directed at James Thompson made him feel good to have survived long enough to see his prodigy grow into this lovely young woman. He thought of her as his child; his reason for being and his reward for having endured the pain of his past.

Gazing out of the car window, Mary Kate picked out the familiar landmarks: the darkening hills; the rocky coast and the flat moor; the heather's early purple flowers bending to the brisk breeze that blew a fleet of little clouds across a high, clear evening sky the colour of robins' eggs.

She sighed happily, "It's so good to be back."

"It's so good to have you back with us." He reached out his hand towards her and she put her hand in his and squeezed it gently.

During the following week the sun shone every day and Mary Kate stayed close to home, helping James in the garden, and in the evenings she would wander down the familiar, rugged path to the shore and sit on a rock dangling her feet in the cool Atlantic water. In the late twilight of evening, she would sit with Sara and James in the drawing-room talking and enjoying each other's company.

On the day she had planned to visit Eleanor Donnelly, the sky darkened, giving way to a rain-storm making the visit impossible. Finding herself at a loss, she wandered upstairs and found herself in the old nursery. She sat in the rocking chair looking at the familiar objects of childhood; the old rocking horse, building blocks, cot and cradle that she remembered so well. Then her eyes wandered to the big shelf in the far corner where sat the dolls house that James had made for her on that Christmas long ago. Getting up, she went over to where it sat, gently running her fingers along its surfaces. She took out each miniature piece of furniture, examining them carefully before putting them back. Memory of that Christmas, of old Jean and Molly crowded in on her causing her eyes to mist over with tears. High up on the shelf, stood her row of dolls; gifts from her mother in New York that had came in parcel after parcel. They looked as new as they day they were purchased, unlike the dolls house, that showed the wear and tear of a much loved and used possession.

She thought of her mother both past and present, as being the bearer of gifts; money, toys, beautiful clothes - "It was you I wanted not your gifts," she said aloud to the emptiness. Taking down a photograph from the top shelf, she carried it to the light of the window. Her mother, stepfather and half brothers stood in a row and behind them a huge house that spoke of affluence and prosperity. Feelings of anger, jealousy and regret seeped into her thoughts as she stared at the handsome smiling faces that seemed to mock her. She thought of the row of beautiful clothes with the Quinn/Laughlin labels that hung unworn in her wardrobe. She preferred to wear the cheap clothes that she had bought herself, with her own money.

Putting the photograph back on the shelf, she went over to the tallboy, casually opening each drawer in turn. In the bottom drawer she removed the sheet of tissue paper that covered tiny hand-made baby clothes. Removing each item carefully she examined them, marvelling at the exquisiteness of them.

She knew that James Thompson's late wife had made them as she awaited the birth of their fist born child.

The tragedy of her death and that of her child struck her forcibly once again. She buried her face in the small garments and as she breathed in deeply, she could smell the faint scent of lavender.

Suddenly the room seemed very dark with all the thoughts and memories pressing upon it. Putting the tiny garments back in the drawer, she replaced the tissue paper and crossed to the mantle where her small oil lamp stood. Striking a match she lit it, watching the warm glow banish the dark shadows.

Sitting back in the rocking chair, she lay looking at the flickering light with a pleasure that was almost untouched by pain.

The rain cleared by mid-morning and she set off for Creega Port. Eleanor appeared from behind the high, stone garden wall to the right of the house as she was making her way along the driveway. "Mary Kate," she said, dropping her basket and giving her a hug. "Come along in and I'll get the kettle on."

They sat in the big kitchen with its terracotta tiled floor and big black range that Eleanor poked into life by adding a few whin sticks and turf. Soon the kettle began to hum as it neared the boil.

"Are you looking forward to teaching at your old school then?" she asked with a smile, putting the tray of tea down on the big wooden table beside Mary Kate, then seating herself opposite.

As she sipped the tea that Eleanor poured for her, she

stared into space for a while. Suddenly, the delight that she had felt on being told about the success of her application seemed to evaporate. What a weekend it had been. A weekend that seemed now like a dream; so sweet, so packed with exquisite experience, it had no relation to the harsh realities of today.

"Well?" Eleanor was probing.

"Sorry, I'm daydreaming. It's just ... well, I've been wondering how the local parents will react to me. My background ... and that'll be common knowledge."

"Nonsense Mary Kate. If you're a good teacher, and their precious wains like you - that's all that'll matter. And I know. And anyway there's nothing wrong with your background."

"You have had a charmed life in many ways Mary Kate. You have been loved and cared for by so many special people."

"I know - I know. But I wanted to be loved by a mother and father like everyone else."

"You have a mother who loves you. She wanted to be a mother to you like everyone else as you put it. Circumstances prevented it - that's all. As soon as she could, she came back to you and wanted to take you back to New York with her, as you well know. But she would have broken Sara and James's heart, not to mention Jean and Molly. And you are far from being the first person to have a father that was as good as no father."

As she listened to Eleanor's recollections of her life,

Mary Kate knew that she would look back on this day as the day when she finally grew up. At twenty-one she was still essentially adolescent, with all the rigid, uncompromising outlook on life, the overwhelming enthusiasms and abrupt withdrawals of adolescence.

In the drawing-room, Eleanor showed Mary Kate the photographs that were a visual recording of her life and times. In the recess near the fireplace, she carefully removed a large, framed photograph from the wall and studied it for a while before handing it to Mary Kate. As she looked at the youthful faces of the handsome young couple, she knew without being told that this was Eleanor and her ill fated, fiancé. "You were so beautiful," she commented. "And so was he - handsome, I mean."

"I should have moved on and found someone else. There were others. But just because I couldn't find an exact replica, I hid away in my grief. Now it's too late. So be warned Mary Kate Quinn. Don't, for God's sake, repeat my mistakes. And don't dwell on the past - grab life with both fists. Blaming others for what we fail to do ourselves is a waste of precious time. I should have learned from my mother's mistakes. When she had a chance at life, she wasted it."

"You have given me a lot to think about Eleanor," she said, handing her back the photograph.

"Maybe too much for one day. And that reminds me.

Secrets on the Breeze

There was a certain young man here looking for you on a couple of occasions. Something about ... taking you to a dance in Clougher Hall on Friday night? I told him that he better look after you, or he would have me to answer to."

"Mike?"

"Aye, Mike. He's good looking. And he's a nice young fellow. Makes me wish I was young again every time I see him. Any-road, I'll tell him you're back, eh?"

"Do. Aye, do." There was an awkward silence between them and to her annoyance Mary Kate could feel herself blush at the mention of Mike.

Half an hour later, Eleanor walked her to the gate, "He has a car now too. A *Wolseley Wasp*, so you'll be going out in style. Will I ask him to pick you up at the Rectory?"

"No. No. Sara and James would faint. Could I meet him here?"

"Surely. If that's what you want. They would soon get used to the idea of you having a boyfriend - they're not that naïve. And I'm sure he's not the first fella in your life."

Mary Kate thought for a minute about her other encounters with the opposite sex; the awkward fumbling of spotty youths in laneways and the love at first sight thing from across the dance-floor that on closer inspection ended in disappointment and disillusion.

Smiling at Eleanor she said, "Aye, a few. But nothing too serious."

On the walk back, Mary Kate was in a totally different frame of mind to that of her outward journey. As she walked along the familiar driveway that led to home, she found that memory was a stronger thing than she bargained for; a sadder and a sweeter thing. She sat down on a flat rock under the Chestnut tree where she had sat with her mother the time when she bandaged her grazed knee. Through the mists of time, she could hear her voice as she sung to her and feel the arms that comforted her. In that instant she decided that she would try on some of the clothes she had sent for the Friday night dance. Getting to her feet, she ran to the back door of the house and went in. Sara and James sat by the kitchen range and she saw her grandmother hastily shove a piece of paper into her apron pocket. She had a strong feeling that they were hiding something; something that they didn't want her to know about.

Chapter 9

Canada

Jean McGregor watched from the window as the police car slowed up and stopped. She watched Mac get out and walk towards her door. She opened it before he had a chance to knock. "Is it OK for me to come in?"

She opened the door wider and nodded for him to follow her.

Sitting down, he lit his pipe before he spoke. "There's a couple of developments concerning the Quinn man that I think you should know about."

"I thought he skedaddled a week ago."

"He did that. But he's back. Back in Mercy Hospital."

"What?"

"Somebody done him over again - nearly as soon as he hit the road."

"Is he badly hurt this time?"

"He's not good. But he's living and conscious and saying he fell. Somebody wants rid of him bad and I'd say it wasn't for his good deeds." Reaching into his pocket he took out a telegram and handed it to Jean. She read it in silence before handing it back. "Seems he won't be welcome back home in Ireland either," she commented, with a deep sigh.

"Wish he had been more specific. Nobody wants to talk when it comes to sexual related attacks on children. And as the law can't deal with it - well then it's summary justice and there's not a damned thing we can do about it."

"What about the New York enquiry?"

"Nothing specific. Just the usual hints and innuendoes," he said, with a shrug of his shoulder.

"The nurses at the hospital say he's been asking for you again. My advice is to stay clear. That's what I came to tell you. Write a note - make whatever excuse you think fit. Just stay clear."

There was a long pause and a deep sigh before Jean answered him. "I suppose you're right. David advised that from the very start. I didn't tell him that I'd been visiting him in the hospital the last time. I thought that I'd saved a life when I found him that evening. Now I'm beginning to wish he'd died. Oh,

Lord - that sounds awful."

"But true," Mac added.

When he had gone Jean sat motionless, shapeless fears flickering through her, like bats fluttering unseen in the night. Going over to the desk, she wrote a short note to the hospital saying she would be unable to visit anymore due to her pregnancy. This done, she resolved to put the miserable business out of her head.

She thought she had succeeded in forgetting about the whole Seamus Quinn affair when the letter arrived from Sara Quinn in Ireland two weeks later. She read, and reread the letter many times until its contents sunk in. It became obvious that this woman was very disturbed at the thought of Seamus Quinn coming back into the lives of the people in her small, rural community. Yet - she was not specific about the reasons why.

Putting on her coat, she went to the bus stop. She felt obliged to show Mac the letter and hear if there had been any new developments.

He looked up from behind the big desk went she when in, a look of surprise on his face. "Sorry to bother you again. But this came," she said handing him the letter. He indicated for her to sit down before he began reading.

"Well, it seems this business isn't going away."

"I feel obliged to answer it. Have you heard anything of him since?"

"You're not obliged to do anything - unless you want to that is. He's left the hospital again. Just up and went like the last time. Only this time he's got his arm in plaster and has a deep wound in his leg that hasn't healed properly. So he won't get too far." He gave her a long searching look before he asked, "Does your husband know about this? Your involvement?"

"He knows a bit about it. But it's something I wanted to do in my own right. I'm bored here and I thought at the time I had done something worthwhile. This man is no threat to me. But I would like to see him prosecuted and I would like to be able to reassure this Sara, that he won't be coming her way again."

"I see. A tall order I'm afraid," Mac replied, with a thin smile.

When she left a few minutes later she felt deflated, refusing Mac's offer of a lift, she walked slowly towards home. She tried to concentrate her thoughts on her unborn child and her plans for her return home. But try as she might her mind wandered back to the letter from Ireland and how she desperately wanted to see justice done.

When David left for work, Jean fell into a deep sleep. It was the sound of the wind that first woke her. It had a deep, hollow whine that came out of the hills and shrieked through the giant pines. Then a tapping sound that mingled with the storm grew louder and a male voice carried by the wind came closer. Jumping out of bed, she opened the curtains and peered outside. He stood hunched up on the doorstep and as he glanced up their eyes met briefly. She stared back at him, frightened and unsure of herself, "My God - John Quinn," she said aloud, as she moved back into the shadows.

Putting on her robe, she made a sudden decision to let him in. When she opened the door, he stared at her in silence for a few seconds before he spoke, "Please ... could I come in for a while? A bite to eat and a rest."

"How did you find me?"

"Saw your address on the nurses notes at the hospital. Please, I'm desperate."

She stood aside to let him pass and as he shuffled past her, she saw that he was trailing his right leg behind him and his right arm, protruding from the grey overcoat was held chest high by a grubby bandage.

He slumped down slowly into the chair by the stove and winched before he closed his eyes tightly. He was overcome by a choking wheezy cough, which left him gasping for breath. Jean collected her thoughts as she busied herself lighting the stove and preparing coffee and scrambled eggs.

He ate in silence, occasioning a wary glace in her direction between mouthfuls.

"I know all about your past," Jean began. "You preyed on children in Ireland, New York, and now here - and God knows wherever else."

The colour drained from his face. He got stiffly to his feet, shocked into rigidity, "What - what are you talking about?"

Fear gripped her for a moment as she watched him stumble forward, his eyes red as he licked his dry lips. Getting to her feet, she stared directly at him and noted the rough stubble that made his face bluish against his pallor.

Suddenly she felt empowered, his appearance diminishing any former threat he may have posed.

"You know well what you have done. The police know what you have done and I know what you have done. If you were thinking about going back to Ireland to escape, I'd forget it. The police there will lift you on sight and that includes the place called Clougher."

He began to shake violently before he slumped back into the chair as sobs shook his body. Jean cleared away the dishes, completely ignoring his distress as she tried to collect her thoughts. She knew that the law could do nothing without witnesses and she must do what she could to prevent him going to Ireland for the sake of the woman who sent her the letter. To her surprise she felt no fear of him and as she glanced at him again she saw a weak pathetic figure.

"I didn't mean ... to do any of this. Seems I would be better off dead."

Secrets on the Breeze

Jean banged the table in front of him, "Shut up. Don't you dare look to me for sympathy - you evil scum. The police are looking for you. I hope they arrest you and that you die in prison. And to think - I was foolish enough to believe I'd done a good deed in saving your life."

He made no reply as Jean eyed him suspiciously. He stood by the stove, his eyes transfixed on a patch of worn linoleum. Slowly lifting his eyes to meet hers he spoke in a hoarse voice, "The only other option I've got - is to get the hell out of here. Go to a mining camp. Anywhere, where there's no women or children."

"It would be better if you gave yourself up."

"Maybe. But, I don't want to die in prison. I have very little time left. They told me at the hospital that I have a shadow on the left lung. TB they say."

Jean gazed at him in silence for a while trying to figure out if he was telling her the truth about his health. True, he looked desperately ill ... but she couldn't be sure. As if reading her thoughts he said, "You don't believe me, do you?"

"Let's face it, truth is not your strong point is it?"

"Maybe not. But this time I'm not lying. I'm no threat to anybody. I just want to disappear and die in peace. I have a wee bit of money saved up - enough to see me out. If you give me a bed for the day to rest up - I'll be out of your way forever by nightfall."

Jean looked at him in silence for a while, unsure of

what she should do.

"Ask the hospital if you don't believe me. Please, just for a few hours to get my strength back." Seemingly exhausted by his pleadings, he slumped back down in the chair and was again seized by a fit of coughing.

"Very well then. I'll make up a bed in the back for a few hours. But you will be gone before David gets home."

"I'll be gone. And thank you."

"I don't want your thanks," she said impatiently before leaving the kitchen.

By nightfall Jean found the room empty, just a vague indent on the bed was the only evidence of his brief stay. Jean breathed a sigh of relief as she closed the door and returned to the kitchen to write a letter to Sara Quinn in Donegal.

Chapter 10

Donegal 1948

June had been blown out like a candle by a biting wind that ushered in a leaden July sky. A sharp, stinging rain fell, billowing into opaque grey sheets when the wind caught it. The hills turned dark grey faces towards a greeny-grey, froth-chained sea that leaped eagerly at the rocks and inlets of the shore. Mary Kate looked gloomily down at the shore and up at the sullen grey sky and groaned despondently before throwing herself back down on the bed, the day ahead stretching before her spelling boredom. Her thoughts went back to Mike and the dance at Clougher. She had walked to Eleanor's to meet him, dressed in one of the beautiful frocks that her mother had sent her.

He looked handsome dressed in grey flannels and a white open necked shirt and her heart raced loudly in her ears as she returned his smile of greeting. He caught both her hands and pressed them gently, "You look beautiful."

"You don't look so bad yourself," she responded shyly.

They drove to the dance in near silence, Mary Kate feeling suddenly very shy in his company.

When they walked towards the hall, they could hear the drone of music coming from the open windows. As they walked through the door Mary Kate could feel all eyes turn in their direction. To Mary Kate's delight Mike was a good dancer and this combined with his charm left her feeling elated.

Later in the cloakroom she met Eileen, a girl she hadn't seen since school.

"I see you're out with Mike tonight," she commented, when the greeting was over.

"Oh, do you know him?" Mary Kate asked in surprise.

"All the girls know Mike. He's been around most of them over the years. A charmer. And he's good looking. Doesn't have much trouble attracting the opposite sex."

Mary Kate brushed her hair and laughed, trying to dismiss Eileen's comments lightly.

"Wonder what happened to the Belfast girl he was

supposed to be engaged to. She probably got sick of his two-timing her."

As she listened, all the pleasure she had felt earlier faded and dwindled into a feeling of humiliation. "Oh I don't know much about him. He just offered to take me to the dance, that's all," she told Eileen, with a dismissive shrug of her shoulder.

Back on the dance-floor with Mike, she smiled and joked as before, while inside all the joy she had felt earlier had disappeared.

When he pulled up at the Rectory gates, his kisses were sweet and his caresses soothed her, and they laughed together, but all the while she knew that she was only one in a long list of foolish girls who had fallen under his spell.

Suddenly he asked, "When can I see you again?"

"I'm not sure. I may go to New York to visit my family. Anyhow, you'll hear from Eleanor ... if I'm around or not."

"Oh, I see," he said, in a wounded tone. When she had kissed him a final goodnight, she could feel the salt tears sting her eyes as she reached the back door and hated herself for being so emotional about someone she barely knew.

During the following days Mary Kate tried to convince herself that Mike's good looks and charm had caused jealousy amongst her friends and that Eileen had perhaps exaggerated or made up the story about his past. But the truth was made real when she saw him driving through the village a few days later with a young blonde girl sitting in the front seat beside him. As she watched she saw them laugh together and as he bent sideways to kiss her, Mary Kate felt as if her heart would break.

Now looking out at the rain, she felt almost desolate in her misery. "If I could have talked to Eleanor about it at least," she sighed, before going downstairs.

In the kitchen Sara stood by the window staring out at the rain seeming lost in her own thoughts. "You all right?"

"Oh, Mary Kate. I didn't hear you come in. Miserable day," she commented, turning around. "The postman has been. He was early today - soaked through poor man. These are for you," she said, fumbling in her deep apron pocket, for the letters. She handed two letters to Mary Kate, then hastily put the other letter back into the pocket, stuffing them deep into the bottom.

"You get anything interesting?" Mary Kate asked.

"A letter from your mother and one from an old friend … in err … Canada." Mary Kate thought she was acting a little strange, as if she was hiding something. She studied her, seeking a clue to what it was. Finally she asked, "Why didn't you tell me about your friend in Canada before?"

"Oh, I hadn't heard from her in ages … and anyway she was away before your time," Sara added dismissively, before turning towards the range and moving a frying pan onto the heat. "Like some bacon and eggs?" she asked, changing the subject. "And by the way … are you planning anything tomorrow?" Mary Kate shook her head. "Yes to the bacon and eggs. I'm always ravenous when I'm at home. But I better cut down on the eating or I'll be the size of a horse."

"Hum … there's not a pick on you. And as for the last few days, you've hardly eaten a bite. I thought you were sickening for something."

"Well if I was I'm grand now … could eat a horse again," she said settling down to read her letters.

"You didn't tell me if you were planning anything tomorrow."

"Nothing much - why?"

"It's just that I was planning on going over to see Grace Murphy in Clougher. Haven't been to see her in a while. And I wondered if you'd make James a bit of dinner?"

"Sure. I can make him something in the middle of the day and then go and see Eleanor."

The following morning began bright and breezy and as she finished dressing, Mary Kate looked out the window and saw Sara heading down the driveway dressed in a bright cotton frock. Her step was light and she seemed happier than she had been of late. She finished dressing and ran down to the kitchen to find James finishing his breakfast. "Yours is in the oven. Sara made it before she left for Clougher."

"I was hoping to catch her before she left," Mary Kate said with a sigh.

"Anything I could help with?"

"Well … maybe. It's about a wee pupil of mine from Dublin, from the orphanage. She cried when I was leaving and I sort of promised her a holiday with us. I should have asked you both first," she added, sitting down opposite him to eat her breakfast.

"Well, I have no objections and I'm sure your grandmother won't either. But, you'll probably have to convince the nuns."

"Aye, I know. I had a letter from her yesterday and she said she had to smuggle the letter out without the nuns seeing it. And she stole the stamp from 'The Mother's' desk."

James whistled before commenting, "a mortal sin if I ever heard one."

"Poor wee thing, she has had a miserable wee life so far."

"What's her name?"

"Sally McPhillips. She's such an adorable wee soul." His watchful eyes held Mary Kate's for a moment before he said with a long low sigh, "Life can be a bugger ... eh? What about you Mary Kate? You seem sort of miserable of late. Boyfriend trouble maybe?" he asked, lifting his eyebrows with a quizzical expression.

She looked at him, at his familiar face that she knew

and loved so well, his candid blue eyes, his sensitive mouth, his grey-brown receding hair and his gentle smile. Suddenly tears came unannounced and she said, "Well, I did meet someone and I thought for a while that he was …God's gift. Anyhow, it turns out I'm only one of many." During the next half hour she confided all her sadness about Mike and he listened intently until she had finished.

At last he spoke, "Poor Mary Kate. Affairs of the heart can be painful. He might not be the heartless fellow you think him to be. But, in either case - in my eyes, he will never be good enough for you," he ended with a grin.

"How did you know … about Mike I mean?"

"Just guessed. You had that faraway look in your eyes and a beautiful young woman like you is bound to attract the opposite sex." He sighed again and spoke as though to himself, "The heart has its reasons, which reason knows nothing of."

Going over to his side of the table Mary Kate bent down and kissed him lightly on the cheek. "What did I do to deserve this?"

"Everything … for listening, for understanding and just for being you."

He patted her on the arm before getting up, "I better get some weeding done."

At the doorway he paused and turned around to face her again, "Mary Kate," he began, "Don't rush into anything with this, or any other man. And remember

I'm always here for you." She continued smiling long after he left the kitchen.

Chapter 11

Mysterious Stranger

When dinner was over she walked down to the
shore and sat gazing out to sea. With a raw hurt in
her breast she tried to put thoughts of Mike out of her
head and instead she thought about her mother.
Fleeting fragments of a greyer and less happy
memory, mingled with smoke and rain came to her
now from the time they spent at the old homestead at
Clougher. Although memory was blurred, she could
recall her own unhappiness in this strange new
environment and knew that she had cried to go home
to Sara, James, Molly and Jean. Now with hindsight
she could feel some of her mother's pain at not being

able to mother her own child. With this new understanding, the resentment she had felt for her mother began to fade and she was seized by an overwhelming need to go back to her mother's old home at Clougher.

Mary Kate walked slowly from the bus-stop towards Clougher village. The warm summer breeze blew lightly against her cheek. She looked across the valley, beyond a spinney of trees unusual in that barren landscape, towards the white cottage built under a cliff as vague memories of the time spent there came and went. She wandered slowly up the village street past the pub, shops and post office, sniffing the scents of fresh paint mingled with smoked bacon and cloves as she passed. With a glance at the church she opened the lynch-gate into the churchyard and strolled aimlessly beneath the shadows of the grey tower towards the main door. She stood there in silence trying not to think of anything in particular and suddenly realised that she felt alone and wondered what she was doing here. It was peaceful in the churchyard and she was suddenly aware of an over-whelming calmness. The very landscape seemed poised as if it were mysteriously waiting, and as she stood motionless, mesmerised by the air of expectancy, she looked towards the village street and saw the figure of a solitary man walking towards her along the brown-grey road that led from the moor.

Secrets on the Breeze

He was tall, wore black and carried a spray of wildflowers. He passed the cottages on the outskirts of the village, and so smooth and effortless were his movements that he seemed to glide down the deserted street. The light breeze lifted his fair hair and ruffled it gently. He walked through the churchyard towards the porch; she was about to emerge from the shadows when he saw her. He must have been surprised to see a stranger in that remote village churchyard. But not even a hint of his surprise showed itself on his face. He looked at her and nodded, "Good afternoon," she said. They looked at each other for a few seconds in silence. She guessed that he was about thirty something, his eyes were blue, wide set, black lashed with an air of mystery and sadness about him.

He nodded, smiled and walked on through the graveyard weaving in and out between the headstones. Walking around the back of the church she watched unobserved from behind the wall as he stood motionless, hands clasped in front of him, the flowers laid beside a new tombstone. She felt like an intruder and walked quietly away.

The mysterious stranger remained in her thoughts as she walked up the hill towards Clougher Burn and the old home that she had come to visit. She could hear footsteps coming from behind her and without turning around she knew that it was the strange young man from the churchyard. She slowed her pace, he quickened his, and they walked along together for a while in silence, "Warm today," he commented. When they reached the crossroads near the top of the hill he said, "I go this way. What about you?"

"I'm just visiting the place. You could call it a walk down memory lane. I spent a bit of time at the old Quinn house when I was very young - just wanted to see if I could find it again."

"I take it you're a Quinn then?"

"Yes. I'm Mary Kate." He held out his hand and shook hers firmly. "I'm Colin Phillips. I'm not from these parts. My grandmother came from here. Two strangers on a summer day," he said, with a slight shake of his head.

"It's been nice meeting you Colin."

She walked a few yards along the road and looked back to find him standing in the same spot. He lifted his hand in a final salute and walked on.

Thoughts of this stranger, and the mystery surrounding him remained with her as she walked slowly towards the farmhouse. In her head she could see those penetrating blue eyes and hear the melodious voice that just wouldn't go away.

When she reached the gateway to the farm she stopped and stood silently gazing and remembering her mother and the sad homesick little girl that she had been. The farmyard sounds seemed to come more sharply to her ears than they would normally have done. Sheep bleated. Someone was playing a tune on a melodeon that had been popular in a war that was just over, the sound of a horse-drawn cart rumbled nearby and suddenly came into view in the laneway. Mary Kate hastily walked on up the lane deciding she was in no mood to meet the new tenants, and begin an explanation about who she was and why she was there.

At the top of the lane she stood in front of a cottage that had recently had a new slate roof put on. She couldn't remember being here before and yet the place seemed disturbingly familiar. She looked uneasily around sensing she was being watched. She shivered. The smallest sounds seemed to be intensified - the sharp crack of a dry twig, the stirring of leaves, the soft flap of a swallow's wing, the small quivering cry of a kitten. Suddenly, she wanted to get away from the place and turned and half ran back down the laneway.

Back in the village her fears subsided and she chided herself for letting her foolish imagination get the better of her, then she remembered her grandmother's reaction when she told her she was going to Clougher. She had seemed startled and uneasy as she exchanged wary glances at James Thompson.

She dismissed the entire episode out of her head as she headed for the small hotel at the end of the street, suddenly realising that she was both hungry and thirsty. Inside, she blinked in the gloomy interior. A young girl at a desk asked, "Can I help you?"

"I'm hoping to get some lunch. Do you do lunches?"

"Aye, come this way," she said walking towards a door on the left. The dining room was brighter and she sat down at a small table by the window. When she was seated, she observed the two middle-aged women sitting at the next table fall silent as their gaze fell on her, making her feel uneasy. When they began talking again she felt herself relax.

When she had ordered lunch she sat gazing out at the church opposite, her mind still on the mysterious stranger she met there. Then from the next table the words spoken struck a chord, "Colin Phillips," "Back at her grave again this morning," one of the women said.

"It's not healthy - grieving that long. I always felt she was unstable and we will never know if she fell off them bens - or jumped."

Just then the waitress brought her lunch and began commenting about the weather. When she finally went, Mary Kate turned her head in irritation straining to hear more, but they had begun to eat in silence. She suppressed a desire to strike up a conversation with the women to see if she could find out more and instead tried to concentrate on the food before her.

When she had paid the bill, she felt compelled to go back to the gravestone where he had left the flowers. She walked slowly over to the grave where the flowers lay on the quiet grass. ***Here Lyeth Henry Fleming,*** *ran the inscription on the tombstone,* ***who died on 8th of October 1902, aged 66 yrs. And that of his wife***

Secrets on the Breeze

Sara who died on the 12ᵗʰ day of April 1907 aged 72yrs. And underneath ran the third inscription, *And that of their grandaughter Rebecca who died on 15th of November 1947, aged 24 yrs.*
This stone was erected to her memory by her devoted fiancé, Colin Phillips. May her soul rest in peace.

She stood still, gazing at the stone as though transfixed, and in her mind she saw again the fair-haired stranger standing with head bent before it and her heart wept for him.

 Out on the roadway she sat down on a rock to wait for the bus. The village was quiet and apart from the occasional passing motor-car, nothing stirred.

Finally the bus arrived an hour late and as it slowly trundled its way along the narrow grey roads, Mary Kate reflected on her strange, mysterious visit to the town-land of her ancestors.

Twilight had come before she reached the Rectory gates and the moonlight came and went between the patchy clouds. Looking at the moon, she imagined that it had a cold white eye that searched into her soul for the secrets she kept hidden there and she wondered how long this strange state of mind would last.

She found her grandmother and James in the kitchen. "I'm glad your back," James said, "We were getting worried when it got so late."

"Oh, the bus was late and as slow as a snail."

"There's hot tea in the pot," Sara said, going over to the range to fetch it.

When she sat down again she asked, "Well did you go into the house? Did you see Ellen and did you call with Grace?"

Mary Kate shook her head, "I intended to. But when I got there I couldn't just walk in. After all I'm a complete stranger to them and they seemed to be busy with the farm-work and that. So I just had a walk around to see how much I could remember."

"Well - did you remember anything?"

"Oh aye, some of it came back to me. Only wee bits of it. When I was there I could only remember the rain and being miserable all the time because I wanted home," she sighed before going on, "Well it wasn't a happy walk down memory lane. I walked on up the lane past the farm and I seen an old house with a new roof. Who does it belong to?"

Sara's face became grave as her eyes darted nervously around the room before she answered. "Ah … that oul' place has been lying empty nearly a lifetime. The man that owned it left for America or someplace. Probably dead by now."

"Who was he?" Mary Kate persisted,

"He was a distant relation of your grandfather's I think." She saw her hands flutter nervously upwards and downwards along her bosom as if pulled by invisible strings. "Enough about that, tell us who else you seen?"

Sensing her unease and unwillingness to discuss the matter further, Mary Kate decided to drop the subject. "Well, I went into the churchyard in Clougher and met a youngish fellow who was putting flowers on a grave. Said his name was Colin Phillips. Would you know who he is?" she asked Sara.

"Not really. But Grace mentioned him to me a few times. He's a bit of a mystery all right - from what Grace says," Sara said, once more, she became her old self, as she went on, "It seems that fellow's fiancés people, on her mother's side came from the area. Anyway she ended up married in Brazil - of all places. The man she married was well off, owned property there and made it rich. Well, the Clougher woman had a hankering for home all the time and he agreed to take her back to Ireland, bought the old Condron Estate and rebuilt the old Manor house, that had been burned down in the troubles in 1921. Anyway, they settled down there and then the oldest son came to live with them for a while. They went back to Brazil and were killed in a plane crash. Their bodies were brought back and buried in the churchyard. The fellow you saw must be their granddaughter's fiancé from Scotland. His grandmother came from Clougher too and got married to a Scotsman. Seems they met in London. She was killed in a fall of the cliff. Poor fella - he doesn't seem to be able to move on and spends all of his spare time with her uncle and his wife who inherited the old place after she died in the fall."

When Sara had finished talking, they sat in silence staring at the glowing turf in the grate. James lit his pipe in silence before saying, "It takes some a lot longer to come to acceptance and move on that others." Mary Kate knew that he was speaking of himself, and his years of drowning his grief in alcohol and her heart went out to him and to Colin Phillips.

Chapter 12

The Parting

When Mary Kate left for her visit to Eleanor, the sun was shining. About half a mile from Eleanor's house, the clouds increased and seemed to press down on the empty sea and overhead the thunder began to echo over the sullen grey hills. She quickened her steps as her apprehension of the pending storm began to grow.

Memories of old Molly, as they cowered in the dark space under the stairs, the sound of her clicking Rosary Beads, the loud praying that increased in volume with every fresh crack of thunder came back to her now.

So great was her fear, she had been oblivious to the car drawing up beside her until she heard the voice, "Mary Kate, jump in quick." Catching her breath, she looked over her shoulder and saw Mike opening the car door for her. "Get in," he urged, just as the rain began in a deluge. Mary Kate obeyed, her heart thundering in her ears. "Get to Eleanor's quick," she urged, covering her eyes with the tail of her blouse, only daring to peer out when the car stopped.

They ran to the door, the knocker only dimly discernable in the half-light as the storm and dusk closed in on them. Out to sea the black mountain of cloud was suddenly split by a brilliant shaft of lightning that flickered over the dark figure of Eleanor, standing in the open doorway. "Get inside quick," she was saying. The crash and roar of the thunder that followed almost instantly half-drowned Mary Kate's cry of terror.

"Please let me get under the stairs - or somewhere," Mary Kate said, fear and panic in her voice.

"It's all right Mary Kate - it's only a thunder storm," Eleanor was saying, "It won't harm you. It will soon pass."

"Please," Mary Kate said, with terror in her voice.

"You really are terrified. Come on then under the stairs," she was saying, leading the way into the hall as she opened the door that led to the dark space under the stairs. "I'd be more scared of the cobwebs in there than the lightning," she commented, as Mary

Secrets on the Breeze

Kate crawled inside. "Go on Mike you can keep her company while I make the tea. I'll call you when it's died down," she said, as she went back to the kitchen. When she regained control of herself, she felt Mike's arms around her, his mouth on her cheek.

"Don't think you can take advantage of my fear. I'm not that far gone," she added. She could hear a chuckle in the darkness as his arms tightened around her.

"Don't," she said, shaking herself free of his grip. "I'm not as free and easy as the blonde you've been driving around with ... or the brunette before that."

"Oh, her. She's just someone I knew from long ago. She was kind of lost here. Knew nobody."

"And you came to her rescue - like The Good Samaritan. Was she your fiancée, or was that another one?"

"You're jealous," he commented, with a laugh. "Suppose that's a good sign."

"It's no sign at all. I'm not interested in your conquests one way or the other."

"Oh, we're playing hard to get."

"No ... just not interested anymore. I suppose with an ego like yours that's unbelievable."

"Hey, you didn't exactly quell my attentions at the dance that night. What's changed?"

"I've got a bit of sense - that's all."

"Well, there's plenty more fish in the sea and I'm not exactly scarce of female company."

"Right ... we understand each other."

"The thunder has moved off now and your tea's ready," Eleanor's voice came from the hall. They scrambled out from the cramped, darkened space into the light and so ended a chapter in their lives.

Later when Mike had gone, she told Eleanor of their brief courtship and the other girlfriends that he had in tow. "I didn't want to rush off and marry him or anything and I admit to being jealous. But he's just a womaniser with a big ego and when he tried to take advantage of my fear - well that just done it."

"I'm glad you found out for yourself Mary Kate. I was going to warn you about him. I only found out about the fiancée and his reputation with women a week ago, when his aunt-in-law came on a visit. And there was me trying to match-make."

"You weren't to know. And anyway, these lessons have to be learned I suppose. But, I admit I thought he was just wonderful and I shed more that a few tears."

"Another wee cup of tea?" Eleanor said, going over to the range for the kettle.

Over the tea Mary Kate told her about her visit to Clougher and her brief meeting with Colin Phillips.

"Oh aye, I heard about him and the death of Rebecca Fleming in a fall.

I taught that wee girl for a while you know. She was a strange wee soul ... kinda sad. She didn't mix much with the other wains. A pretty wee thing, I remember. She had a strange kind of life, hopping about from

Brazil to Ireland and they had a place in Florida too. So I suppose it's not surprising that she seemed strange."

"Poor wee rich girl," Mary Kate commented.

"Aye, riches don't make for happiness in themselves."

"What about the fiancé Colin Phillips? Did you ever meet him?"

"I did once. I went to her funeral. Well, knew her from school and thought I should go. Well, everybody who went to the funeral was invited back to the house for tea. I decided not to bother and I was making my way out the gate when he tapped me on the shoulder. Wanted to know who I was. When I told him, he insisted I went for the tea and he gave me a lift. It was a sad business. Poor fellow was just devastated." Eleanor stared out the window at the rain, seemingly lost in her own thoughts. Then looking back at Mary Kate, she remarked with a quizzical expression, "You're very interested in someone you've just met."

"It was just a strange encounter. A strange day all round and he seemed so sad and intense somehow. Oh, it's hard to explain."

"Did you remember anyone in Clougher?"

Mary Kate shook her head before she answered, "I had wee bits of memory and a strange experience at an old house up the lane from granny's old house. It was an old cottage with a new roof. I had a feeling I had been there before - a feeling of fear that made me shiver like it was haunted or something."

Then looking intently at Eleanor, she asked, "Do you know who lived there and why it's being re-roofed?" Eleanor's heart sank at the question and the look on her face demanded an answer. Why must we all live in this shadow of eternal fear? She asked herself inwardly as she struggled to lie convincingly. "I don't know Mary Kate. Probably been sold to a local. The man that lived there a lifetime ago must be long dead." "Did you know him ... the man that owned it?" Eleanor shook her head and in her eyes Mary Kate recognised that look of unease and fear that her grandmother had shown. "Look, the sun is coming out again. Molly must be looking down on you," Eleanor returned, with a nervous laugh and a tiny cough, which told Mary Kate that she didn't want to discuss the matter further. The wall of silence that had dogged her life was as strong as ever and she simply had to accept it.

On the road home her thoughts went back to the churchyard and Colin Phillips.

Chapter 13

The Visitor

Sara sat down on the hill above the shore and
watched Mary Kate and wee Sally from the Convent,
as they ran across the beach far below.
Her thoughts went back to the day of Sally's arrival.
The shy, brown-clad, little mortal that Mary Kate
brought into the kitchen barely a week ago, bore no
resemblance to the happy child in the blue cotton frock
that ran across the beach with yells of delight.
From the moment she set eyes on wee Sally, all her
mothering instincts took over and she was determined
to win her confidence. What she saw before her now,
was proof of that success and she smiled to herself in

satisfaction.

Sara had painted the walls of the old nursery and made new bright yellow curtains for the windows when the Mother General wrote to say she could spend a three week holiday with them. She knew now that, had it not been for Father Connor's letter, the holiday would not have been possible and they were all determined that it would be a time to remember for this lonely, love-starved child. She was an enchantingly pretty child, with rich, chestnut coloured hair, eyes that matched it, and pale clear skin.

In the evenings, she would steal away to the nursery to play with the toys alone. The dolls house that James had made for Mary Kate seemed to be her favourite. "Have you toys to play with at the Orphanage?" James asked, one evening. She shook her head, "Only on Christmas Day," came the reply.

Sara moved her gaze to the clump of trees to her right and remembered her times of past struggle to survive when Mary Kate was an infant. She remembered the winter when James disappeared and the near starvation that followed. The branches that fell from the clump of trees were the only source of fuel for warmth and she had spent hours breaking and carrying the wood for the fire. In desperation Molly had suggested that she should send Mary Kate back to the orphanage, "At least the wee wain would have food and warmth," she had shouted at Sara. Sara remembered how angry she had become at Molly's suggestion. "She will never darken that door again," she had screamed back at her. Memory of the sad, downtrodden children dressed in identical brown, with heads bent, that she had seen from the Convent window would come back to her and so she had struggled on through that dreadful winter.

Rescue had come in the form of dollars from Maura in America, giving them the means to buy food and fuel for the fire. In her mind she could see herself leaving Mrs Green's shop, carrying flour, sugar, tea, bacon, biscuits, candles, paraffin oil, matches and baby clothes. Driving the pony and trap towards the Rectory gates carrying the goods she could picture Molly and Mary Kate as they waited for her. Those were dark days she recalled, and yet she remembered them and the challenges they posed with satisfaction. When she looked back towards the shore she saw Mary Kate and Sally making their way up the steep path towards her. Dark thoughts about Mary Kate's visit to her old home and the questions she had asked her about Seamus Quinn's house and the new roof sent her spirits into a slump. She hoped she had lied convincingly enough to avoid further questioning on the matter, but she doubted it. As she looked back on her past struggles, the terrible secret of Seamus Quinn was the most painful of all for her and it continued to cause her the deepest anxiety. Her deep love and pride for Mary Kate, was rekindled as she watched her approaching, clutching the small hand of Sally.

"Was it nice in the water?" she asked.

"Cold. But lovely and now we're starving," Mary Kate replied as they flopped down beside her.

"I have saved you some cold chicken and scones for your tea."

Mary Kate smiled at her, a smile that was lighted with affection for the grandmother she loved.

Later, when Sally was safely tucked up in bed, James lit his pipe and pondered again on the cruel nature of humanity. "Fancy them only being allowed their toys on Christmas Day. What the hell kind of a rule is that - as if life hadn't dealt them a tough enough blow by being placed there in the first place."

"She has really blossomed in the wee while she's been with us," Sara commented. "I wish she could stay with us."

James re-lit his pipe and looked intently at Sara in silence for a few seconds before he spoke, "I have a proposal to put to you Sara," he began. "I don't want that child to grow up in an Orphanage and so I have been giving some thought to you and me adopting her. I know we're a bit long in the tooth. But, we have still a lot to give; we could make her happy."

Sara looked at him searchingly for a long time before she answered.

When at last she spoke, the tenderness in her voice was unmistakable. "Don't you think you have sacrificed enough of your life to the care of others?"

"If you're referring to Mary Kate, that was no

sacrifice. More like my salvation. Anyhow, adopting Sally won't be easy. I took the liberty of going over to make enquiries from the Parish Priest this afternoon. Anyhow to cut a long story short, you and me would have to be married and both be of *The Faith*. The age bit wouldn't be important or even what kind of people we were."

Sara looked at him in silent amazement before she spoke, "Oh, James. James Thompson ... you will never cease to amaze me."

"But don't you see Sara. We could be a pair of cut-throats just looking for a slave in our old age, just as long as we were married and were of the right denomination."

"I know James. But your heart is certainly in the right place and that very thought crossed my mind too. We have still a lot to give a wee soul like Sally.

It's just so unfair that we have to be denied the opportunity to make a wee child happy."

Getting to his feet, he paced the floor restlessly for what seemed an age before sitting down again. "Sara," he began, "It's not impossible you know. We could get married and I could take up *The Faith*. I mightn't make the greatest Catholic. But I would do my best."

Sara stared at him open-mouthed, as light began to dawn on her confused mind. "But ... you ... you couldn't make them kind of sacrifices ... it wouldn't be right. Marriage and changing the faith you were brought up with. It wouldn't be right," she repeated with a shake of her head.

"Why not. You and me have been friends for nearly a lifetime and I would trust you with my very life. As for the faith ... well, you know I'm lacking in that department. Not as if I was a devout anything. Come to think of it … I should have married you years ago." Then he looked at her intently for a while before reaching across and taking both her hands in his, "That's if you'll have me Sara. I'm no great catch."

"But if it doesn't work and we don't get the child, then what?"

"What nothing. I'd have done what I should have done long ago. What you and I have had for years Sara, far outstrips the romantic kind of man and woman thing. Nothing will change there, but we will have cemented it in a special way. And we would keep the gossips at bay."

Sara smiled at him with deep affection, "In that case ... how can I refuse. As for the gossips ... I gave up worrying about them a lifetime ago."

They talked late into the night as they awaited Mary Kate's return from the village, half dreading the moment when they would have to tell her about their decision.

When she finally returned, they sat her down and broke the news. They watched her face anxiously and waited. She slumped down on a nearby chair, a look of astonishment on her face. Suddenly getting to her feet, she half ran towards them, "That's the best news ever," she said quietly.

Later when James had gone to bed, Sara and Mary Kate sat in the kitchen drinking tea. Sara had the chance to explained James's visit to Father Connor and their longing to free Sally from the Orphanage. "We could give her a home and make the wee soul happy. But like I said to James, it's not reason enough by itself to take that step ... getting married I mean," she explained.

"It isn't what you think Mary Kate ... James and me. We're not ... ere ... lovers."

Mary Kate watched her grandmother's face redden with embarrassment as she stumbled to explain. "We are just the best of friends and that won't change. People gossiped about us living under the one roof ... especially since Aunt Jean and Molly died. But let them, is what I said."

"Granny, you don't need to explain anything to me. If you had been lovers or not ... makes no difference to me. You two are the most important people in my life and whatever makes you happy, makes me happy."

"I just wanted to explain to you Mary Kate."

"I know Granny. I know and I'm really happy and excited about your decision."

"Well then, so long as you know the truth of it. And don't say nothing to wee Sally in case it doesn't work out. They might think we are too old for a child."

"You're not a bit too old. But I'll say nothing. And talking about Sally - I'm dreading putting her on that train for Dublin, for I know she'll break her heart at leaving us. She can't even take the wee toys and clothes we gave her. She told me they'd be taken from her as soon as she got there."

As she listened, Sara couldn't speak. There was a lump in her throat and she was afraid she might burst into childish tears.

Chapter 14

The Proposition

The days following Sally's departure sent a gloom through the house. The rooms seemed empty and lonely and memories of her heartbreaking sobs as she bid them goodbye seemed to linger in the air.

"I can't bear to go into the nursery since she left," Sara said, as they sat at the big table in the kitchen. James looked at them, the sadness which filled him was the gentle heartbreak that comes of parting. He wished that he had a simple faith in a kind God who moved in a mysterious but scrupulously beneficent way. "We will do our very best to get her back. How could they deny her the right to be in a place where she's wanted and happy?" he asked, getting up from the table and heading for the door.

Five eventless days followed, until each decided to occupy themselves with work in order to forget. Mary Kate went to the schoolhouse every day in order to familiarise herself with the children's workbooks in advance of the re-opening of the school, just two weeks away.

Getting up from the big wooden desk, Mary Kate went over to the window and watched the clouded sky descend low upon the black contour of the hills.

The dark figure of a lone man caught her eye as he moved, blurred and tall in the drizzle. He strode along the crest of the rises on the cliff, lonely and high upon the grey curtain of drifting clouds, as if he were pacing along the very edge of the universe. She watched him climb over the stone wall at the end of the field and it was only when he walked along the roadway towards the schoolhouse that she recognised him. It was the man she had met in the graveyard in Clougher. He disappeared from her vision as he rounded the bend in the lane. Then she heard the creak of the gate and realised that he was coming into the school. Suddenly, he looked up and saw her standing at the window. She went to the door and opened it, "I'm sorry ... I didn't mean to startle you. Just came here on an impulse thinking that the place would be empty. I'm sorry to have bothered you." He made to walk away again. "Wait," Mary Kate began, "Now that you're here you might as well come in."

"Thank you. I'm curious to have a wee look around."
Taking off his wet overcoat he shook it gently and
hung it on the peg in the porch-way before following
her inside. She watched as he walked around the two
classrooms before coming over to the desk where she
stood. "I owe you an explanation," he said in slightly
embarrassed tones. "You see ... my late fiancée was a
pupil here once. I was visiting her grave on the day
we met," he reminded her. "Anyway, I just wanted
to see where she spent some of her childhood. It might
throw some light on … things."

Sitting down on the edge of the nearest desk he bent
his head, running his fingers through his wet hair.
After various random remarks about the weather on
both sides and the lapse of what seemed a very long
time, Colin spoke again, "I need to explain myself a
bit. I'm not sure if I understand myself mind you.
Rebecca was killed by a fall from Benoen Cliff and I
can't seem to move on. Can't get her or the fall out
of my head. So I'm retracing her footsteps every time
I come here." Then he looked at her intently for a
while and said, "Some say she didn't fall … they say
she threw herself off the cliff."

He looked away from her and towards the window,
then turning back to face her again he said, "I'm sorry.
I shouldn't be burdening you with this. I'm so sorry,"
he repeated, getting to his feet.

"Oh, please stay. I'm glad to listen. Just passing the

time here anyway," she added, suddenly not wanting him to leave. "Can't offer you any refreshment I'm afraid. But I've lit a wee turf fire. Just to keep the damp from this rain at bay," she said breathlessly, pointing to the desk chair. "I'll get a chair for myself from the other classroom."

"You sit, I'll get it," he said striding off.

They sat at either side of the fire in an uncomfortable silence for a while. Then Mary Kate asked, "Where did you meet your fiancée?"

"We met at Euston Station in the middle of an air-raid in forty two. I was on leave from the Air Force and trying to make my way home to Scotland. Rebecca was trying to make her way here. Anyhow, we ended up in a shelter together and talked our way through the night. Then we finally got a train and managed to get into the same carriage. We spent that night in Glasgow and I went with her in the morning to get the Derry boat. Well, it was a meeting that sealed my destiny. I fell in love with her there and then. She was beautiful, full of fun and could charm the birds as they say. I came here for the first time to see her before my leave was up. Just had to see her again." The haunted look came back into his eyes and he left her and went to the window, where the rain slid slowly and silently down the glass.

Looking back at her again he said, "I knew her and loved her … yet I didn't really know her. You must think I'm talking in riddles." Mary Kate shook her head, "No, I think I know exactly what you mean."

"She had a dark side you see. Sort of dark moods. Hard to explain it now. But looking back I can see it more clearly. I thought it was the loss of her parents and that. But her uncle told me this dark sad bit ran through the family and that there were suicides in the family way back." He sighed deeply before going on. "That's why I feel this guilt as well as loss. If it was deliberate ... well ... I should have spotted something."

"You shouldn't blame yourself. She was lucky to have had you and known that you loved her so much. And, it probably was an accident."

"Thanks for listening to me Mary Kate. I shouldn't be burdening you with all this. And you're right. I should move on and get on with it. But, I'm kinda haunted by her memory and her uncle Joe has kinda got used to me coming. He waits for me every weekend. Lonely I suppose, poor old boy."

"Anyway, I've talked enough about me and my woes. What about you? Tell me about you"

Under his gaze, she suddenly felt self-conscious and much to her annoyance, she could feel herself blush. "Not much to tell really. I'm a teacher and grew up at the old Redland Rectory. My mother lives in New York. I was brought up by my grandmother."

"No rings?" he asked, glancing at her hands folded on her lap. She shook her head. "I would have thought a beautiful, intelligent girl like you would have been snapped up long ago."

"I met somebody this summer. But lets say … he wasn't what he appeared to be."

"Oh, I'm sorry. But life is a puzzle and people an even bigger puzzle." He sighed again and suddenly smiled at her. His smile was full of warmth and understanding and she found herself wanting this time with Colin to last as long as possible.

Glancing at the window again he said, "The rain seems to have eased off. I'd better be going."

Mary Kate could feel her spirits slump at the mention of his going and she said,

"I must go too. Been here for hours. Not that I have a lot else to do these days."

"In that case I'll help you lock up and we can walk a bit of the way together."

"That'll be grand," she responded, reaching for her coat that hung on the peg close to the fire.

They walked in silence along the wet grassy path with only the cries of the seagulls breaking the silence. "I usually go this way," Colin said, nodding towards a right facing track in the path. "But I'll walk along the lane with you for a bit."

"You don't have to, you know."

"I know that. But I want to enjoy your company a wee bit longer." He suddenly stopped and looked down at her intently for a few seconds. "This morning I felt sad and … well, down at the mouth. But talking to you has perked me up no end. So thanks," he added, with a grin.

As she looked up into his smiling face, Mary Kate, was conscious of a wistful wish that she could take all his grief away and remove forever the haunted sad aura that surrounded him.

"I've enjoyed your company, and I too feel happier than I did when I left home."

"Good," he said, as they walked on. Just past a farm at the bend of the lane, where it was narrow, they had to stand aside for a herd of cattle. They had just come down from Colgan Hill, and the man in charge of them, Johnny Daly, was driving them too fast down the steep brae. They pressed themselves close into the hedge and Mary Kate found herself being bumped and buffeted several times by the fleeing animals. Fearing she would be spun into the lane and trampled by the cloven hooves, she grabbed onto a clump of the hedge.

Suddenly, she was lifted from the ground by Colin and held shoulder high until the last bullock lumbered by and Johnny Daly came panting behind, his stick on his shoulder, his dog at his heels. "Bloody cattle," he said as he passed. "I could shoot them sometimes. I could. Honest."

"A bit late for shooting them. They could have trampled you to death," Colin remarked, still holding Mary Kate high in the air.

Suddenly Mary Kate began to laugh as she looked at

Johnny's lumbering gait disappearing down the lane. "I know they could have trampled us to death. But his reaction was so comical."

"I don't find him a bit funny. Stupid wee man and his bloody cattle," he said angrily, looking up into her face. "Suppose I better set you down again. You know you're as light as a feather," he remarked, as he gently lowered her to the ground.

When they reached the stile, he jumped over in a single bound, slithering a little in the soft mud. He reached for Mary Kate's hand to help her down, his fingers closing on hers, "Stand still for a moment," he said quietly, "You look so … lovely standing there. Makes me wish I had a camera, or better still, was an artist. Look behind you." Turning around she saw that the sky had turned a deep crimson and the dark hills were lathered with frothy clouds tinged with the crimson-red of the sky. "The red fires of sunset. It is beautiful - and if you wish you were an artist, then I wish I was a poet," she added, turning back to face him and suddenly realising that he was still holding her hand.

As she stepped down from the stile onto the soft mud, she heard him sigh softly before saying, "Well, this has to be the parting of our ways and I'm sorry to say goodbye to you." Mary Kate could feel a lump come into her throat and felt she couldn't trust herself to speak, so she just smiled. Bending down, he pressed his cheek against hers. "Thank you for helping a wandering, lost soul in his hour of need." His voice sounded broken and pained. Much to her embarrassment, her eyes filled suddenly and a short shower of tears rolled down her face. She wiped them away roughly, hoping he hadn't noticed.

When she felt in control of her emotions again, she said, "Goodbye Colin. I hope you find ... happiness again. And you will - in time."

"Thanks Mary Kate. You have a kind heart," he said, and he told her so by taking her hand and raising it formally to his lips. His eyes were so sorrowful now. He walked away a few paces, then turned around towards her again. "Mary Kate - could we maybe go out for a drive or something sometime? I'll be back in a couple of weeks or so. I'll send you a note - let you know."

"Right. I'd like that." They smiled at each other, then he turned away and moved towards the cliff path. At the crossroads, Mary Kate stopped, looked up, and saw far off on the hill, lonely and dark against the yellow evening light, the strange and lonely figure of Colin Phillips.

The days following her encounter with Colin were strange, restless days for Mary Kate. Memory of him seemed to fill all her waking thoughts to the point of near obsession. His melodious voice with its Scottish lilt, echoed in her ears and images of his sad haunted appearance remained in her memory like a series of photograph images.

Hazel McIntyre

On dry days she went to the school or called with Eleanor Donnelly or just wandered around the house from room to room. "What's wrong with you these days. You seem lost in a world of your own?" Sara asked.

"Nothing's wrong. Just a wee bit anxious about the new job," she lied.

"Well, so long as you're not sickening for something." Mary Kate was always a believer in common sense, in theory if not always in practice. She told herself repeatedly that falling for a man who was grieving for his dead fiancée was the height of folly, and that his only interest in her was for a ready listening ear and a shoulder to cry on. Then she would remind herself about Mike and all the sorrow that her ill judgement about his character had brought her. But there was also a part of her mind, which was always escaping from her control and playing tricks; fixing on her memory romantic images of this man she hardly knew, and then haunting herself with them.

Mary Kate wandered into James' old study in search of a book, hoping she could take her mind off waiting for the post and being disappointed when the promised note from Colin didn't come. Two huge parcels had arrived from her mother that morning and she had tried to share Sara's excitement at opening them and admiring the contents of clothes, shoes, canned foodstuffs, chocolate, coffee and an endless array of small items that had been carefully chosen by her

159

mother. She tried on the winter coat and it fitted her perfectly and she loved its plum colour. "It's lovely on you Mary Kate," Sara had said, "But then a beautiful bride's easily dressed, as they say. And, talking of brides; ones that are a bit long in the tooth that is, your mother is sending me the outfit. Nothing fancy, I told her. I don't know how we would have managed during these war years and rationing, without your mother's parcels." She had listened with half an ear, making her escape to her room with the excuse of putting away her mother's gifts.

Now in James's study she went through his book-shelves, trying to concentrate on finding something that would interest her. Her gaze wandered absently to the cupboard- door at the end of the shelf of leather-bound books. "A room without books is like a body without a spirit," James used to tell her when she was a child. Reaching for the door handle, she turned it and much to her surprise it opened with a reluctant creak from its hinges. As the door was always locked in the past, the exploration of its interior was all the more interesting. On the far wall she removed an old sheets from a group of canvas paintings. Some were portraits and some landscapes. In the gloomy light she could make out a portrait that resembled herself. She carried it carefully to the study window for closer inspection and to her amazement it was unmistakably her own image that emerged from the canvas. Puzzled, she went back again and again, until she had removed all the paintings for examination from their dark hiding place. "James has to be the artist," she whispered to herself in amazement as the sheer excellence of the work almost took her breath away. One portrait in particular, captivated her and left her puzzled. She thought she recognised the woman in the portrait and then changed her mind. Using one finger, like an impresario, she ran it gently across the canvas and then stood at a distance surveying it. One moment she thought it was her grandmother and the next his dead wife. She ran across the landing and into her own room, where the portrait of his dead wife hung on the far wall. She stood still and surveyed the image for a few minutes, and then going over to her dressing table, she picked up the photograph of her grandmother and rushed back to compare the images with the painting. Suddenly, it became clear; he had painted portraits of the two women in one. She was so engrossed in what she was doing, she didn't hear him come into the room. "What do you think you're doing?" he almost shouted from the doorway, "This is the only room in the house that I claim for my own. The only bloody room."

Mary Kate stood a few feet from him watching him with round fearful eyes.

"I'm sorry. I … I didn't mean to pry. I just came in for a book and … and sort of absently tried the door. When it opened I couldn't help looking at … at these," she stammered, nodding in the direction of the paintings.

He stood still and stared at her angrily before crossing the room to where she had stood the paintings. "They are lovely ... you are so talented." Mary Kate's voice snuffled and her voice wobbled. James glared at her with anger in his eyes. She stood there like a cumbersome child, her eyes tear-filled and her mouth trembling. "I'm sorry," she sank her voice to a whisper, "I should have respected your ... your private things."

He took his gaze away from the paintings and looked at her in silence for a while, "You always were a wee nosey parker." The anger had suddenly left him. He sat down on the chair behind the desk and indicated for Mary Kate to sit down opposite. He sighed deeply, then rose from the chair again and went into the closet, returning with another canvas wrapped in a piece of white cloth, "You've missed the best one," he remarked, carefully removing the cloth from the canvas. "Recognise anybody?" Mary Kate stared at the portrait that he held out for her inspection. The face was that of a small child with dark soulful eyes and hands that appeared to stroke an invisible object. "That was you. The you - that rescued a drowning man."

"I'm not ... not sure what you mean."

Moving back to the chair behind the desk again, he sat down facing her. "I had a stroke once," he began, "And I wanted out - away out of the hell that was my life. I drank myself into near oblivion for years and the old body reneged I suppose. Anyway, your grandmother refused to grant my wish and end it for me. Instead she brought you - sat you on the bed beside me and walked away.

Your small chubby hands stroked my face, 'Better soon,' your small voice repeated over and over. I don't know what happened to my desperate thoughts. But from that moment on - I fought back." He drew in a deep breath, and the look that he directed at Mary Kate had become soft and gentle, gone was the earlier anger and hostility.

"The paintings," she reminded him, "Why did you hide them away?"

"I was coming to that. An alcoholic doesn't change his spots too easily and I was no exception. I had relied on the drink to create a sort of amnesia ... to sleep, to just use as a crutch. Anyway, the stroke meant that if I carried on drinking, I'd pop the clogs pretty quick." He sighed deeply, his gaze moving from her face, to the row of paintings.

"Well, I began searching for a winter pursuit - to take my mind away from the constant need of whiskey. The first portrait I did was the one of you. Tried to capture the wee face that was my salvation ... so to speak."

"They are lovely - every last one. They shouldn't be hid away in a dark cubby-hole, they should be displayed in a gallery," Mary Kate ventured, her eyes searching his face for a reaction.

"No. These are my secret - at least they were until you came nosing around."

"Sorry again. I promise that I will never pry again. But I wish I could have one."

He raised his eyebrows before he asked, "Which one?"

"I love them all. But this one is the most powerful image," she said, going over to the portrait of the woman. "Who is she?" she asked.

Mary Kate gazed at him with a surge of regret for having asked as she watched him stand up, turn around and stare at her with a look of sudden rising annoyance. He gazed at her long and hard before he answered, "That was done years ago and I suppose it ... it represents the two loves of my life. My late wife - and your grandmother. Do you know that you are a nosey-parker Mary Kate? Come to think of it you always were."

Mary Kate eyed him with a certain amount of caution, and when she saw him smile she ran to where he stood, flinging her arms around his waist, "It's the first time I've ever seen you mad at me."

They sat down again and when he had lighted his pipe he said, "See the painting of you - I intended to give it to you on your wedding day. But you've spoiled it now."

"I'm sorry. But as I won't be going down the isle for a long, long time, or maybe never. Could I have it now?"

"You have a brass neck, Mary Kate Quinn. But I suppose you can take it with you."

"I will treasure it forever," she said with emotion in her voice.

"I think that you will find the love of your life sooner than you think. And whoever he is, he will be a lucky man. What about this Mike fellow? Is that all off?"

"Aye, long ago and I'm better rid of him." This gave her the opportunity to tell him about Colin Phillips and when she had finished, he stared out the window in silence. Finally he spoke, "This is a difficult one. Somebody who is pining for his dead fiancée could spell trouble. I suppose I'm a prime example of this … ask your grandmother."

"I'm not falling for him. I just wanted to tell you about him, that's all."

"Good … good. Mind you, you seem taken by him if you ask me."

His eyes twinkled at her through the smoke from his pipe, as it swirled around his head. "I'm not daft James Thompson … one romantic disaster in one summer is enough for anybody."

"You can put my paintings back where you got them and we'll go down for some tea."

Chapter 15

The Flowers

Mary Kate cycled along the quiet laneways, on her first day as teacher at Clougher School. Her emotions were a mixture of excitement and apprehension as she contemplated the new challenge. When she reached the school gate, she stood and gazed at the familiar scene and her thoughts went back through the mists of childhood, remembering the first time she walked through these same gates clutching James Thompson's hand. She reached the big brown door, and as she fumbled for the key the bunch of flowers caught her eye. Bending down, she picked them up and hastily read the note that was attached,

'Thinking about you on your first day. Good luck. Hope to see you again soon. Colin'

She stood staring at the note for ages, lost in her own thoughts. Suddenly, she felt a glow of happiness flood through her. "He hadn't forgotten me after all," she whispered, as she unlocked the big door of the schoolhouse.

When the children started to arrive, there was little time for thoughts of Colin Phillips. They eyed their new teacher with curiosity and she felt nervous as she looked down on the sea of young, unfamiliar faces. But as the day progressed, she felt obliged to stamp her authority on the class and much to her delight they soon settled down to work. By the end of the first week, she was able to put a name to almost all their faces and on Friday afternoon, as she read them the first chapter of *The Secret Garden* she felt that she had accomplished a trust between herself and her pupils.

During the weekends Mary Kate wandered along the cliffs still hoping to catch a glimpse of the lonely figure of Colin Phillips in his solitary wanderings.

She wanted to find out what it was really like to be in love. She wanted to be in someone's arms and lose herself in the delight of his kisses. When she looked back on the nights she had spent with Mike, it seemed to her absurd, empty, worthless. If that was 'love' why did poets sing of it? Why did women pine for it? Why did it drive James Thompson to drink and near madness? With Colin Phillips it might be different. In spite of all the warnings, she wanted to find out.

Chapter 16

He Walks the High Hills

Colin Phillips wandered across the sodden grass to the grave and laid a bunch of purple heather under the headstone. He had been too well aware of the perils of getting engaged to a girl as deep and strange as Rebecca Fleming. The strange force of Rebecca's love had borne him away from his previous self. The vivacious, happy-go-lucky side of Rebecca was the Rebecca that he first knew and fell in love with and he would have agreed to anything so long as he was with her. The dark, cold and silent side of her nature he had dismissed at his peril, leaving him ridden with guilt by her death.

Was it indeed suicide, like the whispered comments of the local people suggested? And if so, why had he not known about her mental turmoil and done something to prevent her death? Why hadn't he realised how serious her mental state had been? She'd had dark moods all the time he knew her and now looking back, he had accepted them as part of her personality.

He should have moved on long ago he told himself, as did his own family back home. But he didn't really want to leave the place that he now thought of as home. During the war years the place had become his escape from the terrors of war, the dying, bombings, the ever-present fear that each day could be his last. Walking the heather-clad hills alone had given him the peace and hope he had needed and now he couldn't walk away from it.

Thoughts of Rebecca were of late mingled with those of Mary Kate. Her face would loom up before him unexpectedly and this brought feelings of both joy and guilt. He had a vision of her now sitting in the quiet schoolroom, her brilliant brown eyes filled with sympathy as he talked about his grief for Rebecca. It seemed so long ago, a lifetime, he had stepped across a great divide that morning, a chasm he had only dimly recognised at the time but which he now knew to be of vital importance in his life. Guilt and Rebecca's memory kept him at a distance from her, but as he watched her from the high rock as she cycled to school, had made him realise that his feelings were too strong to fight any longer. He wanted to ask her out to a dance and get to know her better.

He walked up the driveway like a dark ghost in his black coat. The moon was rising early over the sea, peering at him like a curious neighbour. The skeletal trees whispered together in the cool breeze. "I will have to tell Rebecca's uncle about her," he thought. "Is there anything to regret in this? I could not live with myself if I pretended to live a lie, wandering the hills with Rebecca's ghost forever." He stood at the gate, staring at the dark shape of the big grey house. The wind blew troubled clouds across the sky and he breathed deeply, wondering if it was the last time he would stand there again. Then he walked around to the back, opened the door and went in.

Joe sat in the small drawing room to the right of the hallway, the smoke from his pipe rising high above his head making his outline ghostly in the fading light. "It's you Colin," he said hoarsely when he saw him sit in the chair close by.

"Where've you been?"

"Oh, just walking and thinking."

The old man looked at him intently for a while before he asked, "Well, did you reach any decisions?"

Colin nodded. "I suppose you could say that I'm weary of letting the world pass me by."

"So you've decided to re-join it … so to speak."

"I have in a manner of speaking and I want you to be the first to know."

"I've met a girl. Never thought I'd be interested in another woman after Rebecca. But I can't go on living like a recluse forever."

"Well, I'm glad for you. Like you say, you can't go on forever living in the past." His tone pierced him with compassion and as Colin looked at him in the flickering firelight, he thought he looked so old and sad, his skin like ageing parchment over his bones. "Tell me about this girl. Is it serious?"

"Wait a minute. I barely know the girl and I haven't even asked her out with me yet. It's just that I wanted you to be the first to know that I'm thinking about asking her. Seen her for the first time in Clougher churchyard. Then again at the wee school where she is going to teach. Her name is Mary Kate Quinn."

Colin was amazed to see Joe's face light up and a broad grin creep across his face. "You mean she's a local girl? And there was me thinking you'd found someone back in Scotland, or somewhere and were saying goodbye to me."

Colin shook his head, "You won't be rid of me that easy … that's unless you want to see the back of me."

"Nothing could be further from the truth. I've come to rely on you over these years. I miss you every time you go and wait patiently for your coming back. The loneliness of old age, I suppose. I wanted you to find a nice girl for a long time.

But I selfishly didn't want to lose you. You see …
you are the only one I have left and I look on you as
my own."

His eyes on the darkening-hazed horizon, Colin saw
the red-orange glow of the fading light and
remembered Rebecca, the clash of conflict long since
silenced on the shores of time, wondering if loss was
the reason and the essence of the world. Turning to
Joe, he spoke with emotion in his voice, "I'll be here
for you for as long as you want me to."

Getting up stiffly to his feet, Joe went over to the
sideboard, "Let's have a wee jorum before we eat,"
he said, pouring whiskey into two glasses.

Upstairs, Colin made to go to his own room to change,
thought better of it and found himself in Rebecca's
room instead. He absently opened one of the
wardrobes and ran his hand along the row of dresses
that hung neatly as she had left them. A black satin
evening dress brought back a vivid recollection of
her wearing it on that night in London. They had sat
opposite each other in a restaurant in silence and try
as he might he couldn't cajole her out of her dark
mood as she shifted the food idly around on her plate.
"Not hungry?" he had asked. She shook her head
and stared into the distance. "What do you want life
to give you, Rebecca?" he had asked.

"More than I have had so far. I want a reason for
being but I've never found one yet. My father used
to say that God was the reason, but he perplexes me.

Secrets on the Breeze

He can't be a cause for living and a cause for dying - there's too much he does not answer. Ask - and every time you come up against a wall of his silence. Take no notice of me Colin ... one of my dark days."

As they walked back along the strand, her mood lifted and she became once more, the charming, happy Rebecca he had fallen in love with.

Now as he stood in her room and looked around at her one-time possessions covered in dust and swaying cobwebs, he decided it was time to move on.

Chapter 17

The Invitation

Colin Phillips stood on the heather-clad hillside, in sight of the schoolhouse until he saw the children run through the gate, their voices carried upwards in the still air. Then he saw her, walking out to the yard and through the gate. He ran down the path and onto the laneway, just in time to catch her, "Mary Kate, Mary Kate," he called after her. Turning around she saw him and smiled.

"Colin. I didn't expect to see you. Thanks for the flowers on my first morning. It was very … very thoughtful of you."

"Oh it was nothing. Just a wee gesture of my thanks.

Secrets on the Breeze

Can I walk a bit of the way with you?"

She nodded and they walked along in silence for a while. "Have you no bicycle today?" he asked.

"It's punctured. James brought me here in the trap this morning."

"You would need a motor car for the winter," he remarked.

"I can't drive and anyway motors cost money. Teachers' pay is very bad, you know. Have you a motor car?"

"I do. But when I come here, I prefer to walk. Just love to wander the hills alone." He stopped suddenly and said, "Mary Kate, would you come out with me one night? We could maybe go up to Derry, to the cinema and have a meal or ... or whatever you want?"

His question sent Mary Kate's thoughts into confusion. She had dreamt of the day when he would ask her this question, and yet she was wary of being swept into his lonely world, his life, his grief, his loss and his lonely wanderings.

She looked up at him and saw a lost, almost pleading expression on his face.

Before she had a chance to reply he said, "I know you are wary of me. I must seem like a strange recluse wandering the hills in search of the ... the dead. But I've put the past behind me. Rebecca will always be a part of my past. Nothing more than that - I made sure of that before I asked you out."

"All right then - a night at the pictures would be great."

He smiled at her in relief, "Good, I was afraid you'd turn me down. How about tomorrow evening? Last day of the week, and that."

"Right. That'll be fine."

"I'll pick you up at the house about half six."

She nodded feeling suddenly self-conscious, "Right … I'll be ready."

He reached for her hand and pressed it gently. "I told old Joe about you. Rebecca's uncle," he added, noticing the puzzled expression on her face.

"He has invited you to tea sometime. I felt I owed him honesty, you see. He's a lonely old man who has lost so many of his family and I feel a sort of obligation to him. He's been good to me. Anyway, when I told him he was pleased that you came from here and that I wasn't going to disappear on him."

When they reached the steps that led to the short cut, he took her arm and helped her across. "You don't have to go to see old Joe - just though I'd tell you," he said.

As she watched him jump down from the steps, Mary Kate wondered about the old man in that big, lonely old house and apart from Colin's weekend visits, only the ghosts of the dead for company. "I'd like to visit him sometime. He must be lonely," she said, suddenly reaching a decision.

"Good. He'll be delighted to welcome you." She met his eyes. "He must be very fond of you," she said softly.

Secrets on the Breeze

He took in a deep breath. "He's become dependant on me - I suppose. Too much sorrow and loss in his life - nobody should have to be as lonely as he is."

He smiled and reached down, touching her cheek. "Out of interest, what were you doing in the graveyard that day?"

"It's a long story. I suppose you could say I was taking a walk down memory lane. I spent some time with my mother in the Quinn house in Clougher Hill when I was about three. I just wanted to see how much I'd remember from that time." She looked away towards the darkening hills before she spoke again. "Exorcizing old ghosts, you might say."

"So - you have those too."

"Aye, too many of them," she said, sighing.

"Whatever took you there, call it fate, whatever. I'm glad we met, for I was drifting like a feather in the wind. And from that day in the school, you have been in my thoughts all the time."

"There's a lot about my past too," she began, suddenly wanting to tell him everything, to get her past out in the open.

"My mother went to New York, shortly after my birth. She is married there now and I have two half-brothers, I barely know. As for my father - well I don't really know who he is. My grandmother brought me up."

When she had finished, she felt foolish and angry with herself for telling this man she barely knew about her past.

When she looked back at him, she could feel her face redden, "I'm sorry. I'm sure you don't want to hear all ... all this family history."

Colin's eyes had a sober intensity. "I'm gad you told me. Secrets can fester away and destroy us. Now we are quits eh? I burdened you will all my dark shadows too, you know."

"Now we're quits eh? Two ships in the night with no secrets between them," Mary Kate said, her eyes danced dark and teasing and Colin laughed back at her. Colin's eyes fixed on her face, that look in them again that she couldn't quite fathom. Then reaching down, he cupped her face in his hands and kissed her on the lips, "Till tomorrow night."

Chapter 18

New York 1947

Maura Quinn sat quietly looking out at the trim
green lawn fringed with the gold russet of the autumn-
leafed trees, Mary Kate's letter clutched in her hand.
The long letter from Mary Kate came unexpectedly
and its content brought back dark echoes from her
past, a past that she for the most part was able to keep
from the forefront of her mind. It was the vivid
description of Seamus Quinn's old house, and her
daughter's vivid description of her feelings of menace
and foreboding, that had made her heart lunge heavily.
"Will this ever go away?" she whispered into the
silence, putting the letter down on the table in front

of her and lighting a cigarette with a tremor in her hands.

Looking back at the letter again she made an effort to recall all the cheerful, happy bits of news: her new job; the young man in her life; how well her new clothes fitted and the plans for her mother's wedding. But it was her description of that cottage and the fearful memories that it conjured up that left her feeling almost in a state of collapse. When the phone rang the sound of it went through her with an excruciating shock. She sprang to her feet, tipping the chair over with a crash and stared at the telephone as if it were a strange and dangerous enemy.

Picking up the receiver she said "Hello," her own voice sounding small and strange.

"Hello sweetheart. You sound funny. Everything all right?"

She breathed a sigh of relief at the familiar sound of Andrew's voice, "I'm fine. Just feeling a bit tired today, that's all," she replied, trying to sound casual.

"Well you just stay put then; take a nap and we'll go out to dinner when I get home. You work far too hard, you know."

"I'm fine honey, honest," she added, putting as much cheer into her voice as she could muster.

When she hung up, she went into the drawing-room and sat down on a long, cream sofa. Her eyes took in the elegant grandeur of the room, from the pale grey drapes, to the warm glow of the restored wood, the old paintings, the lavish, ornate chandeliers and fine carved furnishings all spoke of her present affluent lifestyle. A large framed painting of herself, smiling and serene, hung above the mantle. It had been a Christmas gift from Andrew, painted from a photograph taken a few years earlier.

She thought about her two fine, strapping sons, on vacation at the log house in the mountains. A place of brilliant lakes and fresh smelling pine trees, a place with a nostalgic frontier feel about it, a world away from the shadowy, memory of the cottage that had so disturbed Mary Kate back in Ireland.

Yet nothing about her present life could alleviate the pain or the memory of her early adult life, she had reconciled herself to that destiny long ago.

The long letter from Mary Kate puzzled her from the moment she felt its bulk inside the envelope. For many years, her daughter's correspondence had been brief, said little about her true feelings, and seemed simply a duty undertaken only when absolutely necessary and Maura read resentment between each line.

It had taken years to resign herself to the fact that she could never have that close mother-daughter relationship that they both longed for. How could it be otherwise, when they lived thousands of miles apart and this left Maura with deep feelings of guilt and longing. But she also knew that the circumstances of her birth must always be kept from her firstborn, she must never know that she was a child conceived of rape and by keeping that knowledge from her, Mary Kate would never understand why her mother was forced to be much less than a mother should be.

She went back to the window and stared out at the sunlight that glinted in the leaves of the big maple tree on the lawn.

Memories of that awful time when she had been forcibly shipped to New York like a piece of baggage in order to save the family name came out of the dark shadows of her memory, causing her to shiver slightly. Often looking back, she wondered what would have become of her, had she not met Andrew Jefferson? She would most likely have been a servant in some smart area of the city, living out her life quietly serving others more fortunate.

Andrew had been her salvation and his love never ceased to amaze her, even after all these years. To her employees at her three stores and to the world in general Maura presented an efficient, good-humoured manner and this was her defence against her low self-esteem and secret fears that were the scars of her past. Many times over the years she had thought she saw Seamus Quinn, leaving her fearful and shaking. The episode in the bank yesterday evening now came back to haunt her. Her partner Hanna, who usually dealt with the banking end of things, was held up at a fashion show. She had parked the car and walked along the street towards the bank when she saw him.

Secrets on the Breeze

He wore a black leather windbreaker and a black scarf wrapped tightly around his throat. In spite of his limp he moved swiftly, and silently and only the white flash of his face was visible in the yellow street lamps. Something about him made her heart quicken and her throat tighten in fear. When he disappeared inside the high door of the bank building, she managed to pull herself together, reassuring herself that it was only an illusion of her imagination as before.

"Seamus Quinn is thousands of miles from here and probably long dead' she whispered, as she forced herself to walk steadily into the bank behind him.

Standing in the queue behind him, Maura felt that she had her nerves under control as she watched the cashier move away from the counter apparently consulting her colleague with occasional nods back in the direction of the man in the black windbreaker. Suddenly he looked around and for a brief second their eyes met. Maura could feel the sudden lurch of her heart as she looked into the dull, wary eyes that stared back at her. She noticed the deep scar under his left eye and the dirty bandage that showed above the scarf. All her muscles tightened spasmodically as she stared at the figure before her. For an instant neither of them moved; standing perfectly still they stared at each other, their breathing a slow labouring sound in the silence. "Next please," the clerk at the next counter said. Maura moved away from him, trying desperately to regain her composure, handing over her bags that contained the day's takings. The clerk eyed her curiously, "Are you OK Madam?" "Yes, yes fine," she stuttered.

As she was leaving she glanced at him again and noted the large sum of cash being counted out before him. Once outside, she half-ran to her car, unlocked the driver's door and got in. It was then that the weakening fear hit her and she began to shake, as blisters of sweat broke out on her forehead. Gripping the steering wheel tightly, she watched him limp from the bank using his right arm to hail a taxi. She noticed the yellow, old-parchment colour of his face and the stooped, aged appearance. "It can't be him. He is too old. I'm just letting my imagination run wild again," she whispered to herself, as she watched him, and yet she knew that there was a frightening familiarity about him. Seeing a cab coming towards him, he limped impatiently towards it. As Maura continued to watch him, a car seemed to suddenly appear from nowhere and as it struck him, she saw his body being thrown into the air and landing heavily on the hard surface of the road. Maura covered her eyes for a few seconds and when she looked again the form on the ground was surrounded by a mass of people. Getting out of the car she walked slowly towards the crowd of people surrounding the man on the ground, then finding a space between them she looked down at the still, silent form on the ground. The yellow, old parchment colour had faded from his face, his skin was now a dirty grey, his eyes were closed and blood trickled from his mouth. The long, low whail of an ambulance sounded and as it came closer people moved away to the sidewalks. A policeman came towards her and asked "Did you see what happened mam?"

Maura swallowed the dry constriction in her throat, "No ... no. I saw nothing," she said hoarsely.

She went back to her car and watched the ambulance crew lift him into the ambulance and move away at speed, its sirens wailing in urgency.

As she drove towards home she decided to remain silent about the episode to Andrew, he had suffered enough already because of her past fears.

Now alone in the house her nerves were strained to almost breaking point. She was caught again in the hopeless web of fear and guilt, love and hate. The telephone rang again and she breathed a sigh of relief when she heard her friend and business partner's cheerful voice at the other end, "Andrew just called. He's worried about you, he says you're not well."

"Oh, I'm fine. Just a wee bit tired is all. He fusses too much," Maura said, trying to sound as cheerful as possible.

"Look, why don't we go out for a bit of lunch? I'll pick you up in twenty minutes or so," Hanna added, before Maura had time to respond.

"Tell you what, come to the house and I'll make us a

sandwich."

"Right then. See you in a while."

When she had put down the telephone, she thought about her long friendship with Hanna. They had first met on the voyage to New York where they shared a cabin and the bonds of friendship between them continued to endure.

She had the sandwiches and coffee ready when Hanna pulled into the driveway.

"What's wrong Maura? Out with it. I know you well enough to know when something's bothering you."

Maura told her about Mary Kate's letter at first and went on to tell her about the incident in the bank. In the silence that followed, Maura stared at her friend, conscious of the labouring beat of her heart in the stillness of the room. A wind from the river caught the lace curtains, blowing them into the room and toppling a vase from the low table, the sudden crack, as it reached the floor was sharp and loud in the silence.

"Have you told Andrew?" Hanna asked quietly. Maura shook her head, "He has heard enough of my fear of the unknown to last a lifetime. No … no I'm not bothering him with any more of it."

"Seems to me that he senses something anyway. This man in the bank … what made you think it might be him?"

"Something about him. Then when he looked at me … well, I saw the fear in his eyes."

Secrets on the Breeze

"Oh Maura, come off it - be realistic here. This is a city of … of millions. The coincidence of seeing him here is millions to one."

"I know. I know. But I'm still half - convinced that it was … was him."

Maura stared out the window in silence, struggling in her mind to push away the image of Seamus Quinn, the eyes that looked so frighteningly familiar, the blood trickling from his mouth, the grey pallor of his face as he lay on the ground.

"Look Maura, why don't you find out which hospital they took him to and if he is dead or alive." Maura shook her head, "I'd be terrified of what I might find out. And I lied to the policeman when I told him I saw nothing. I seen it all happen, the car that struck him - everything."

"Do you want me to find out for you? I can make a casual enquiry from the bank staff to start with. It might set your mind at rest. In fact I know it will as there's as much chance of the man you saw being Seamus Quinn as of me going to the moon next week," Hanna added with a grin.

"I wish I was so sure. You think I'm losing my marbles don't you?" she asked, her eyes suddenly filling up.

"No. No, no Maura. You know me better than that for God's sake. If I had been a victim of that scum, I'd probably be the same as you."

Going over to the drinks cabinet Maura poured gin

into two glasses and added some tonic-water. "Here, drink this it's great stuff for the nerves."

When the first warmth of the gin flowed through her body, she felt better immediately, willing at once to find out if the man she saw really was who she dreaded and then forget the incident ever happened.

"Hanna, will you try and find out for me. I want to know so that I can put him and all that he stands for behind me."

"That's more like it," Hanna said with a broad smile. "You have far more courage than you give yourself credit for. Now, go and get yourself glamorous for that good looking man of yours."

At the door Hanna said, "You will have nothing to worry about. I'll let you know tomorrow if I find out anything. But it won't be him, of that I'm sure."

Later that afternoon, Hanna went to the bank with the shop takings as usual.

"Well, it seems I missed all the activity yesterday," she commented to the clerk. "The accident outside," she added, noting the puzzled expression on the girl's face.

"Oh that. The guy was in here just seconds before and the next we heard was the screech of brakes."

"Was he killed?" Maura asked, tentatively.

"I heard he died on the way to hospital. An Irishman, the cops said. They were in here earlier asking if we seen anything," she added by way of explanation.

Secrets on the Breeze

"Poor man," Maura said, "Don't happen to know his name?" She shook her head, "Sorry."

As Hanna walked down Thirty-Fourth Street, her thoughts were on the man who had been killed two days ago. She needed to find out who he was, and if by any wild stretch of the imagination Maura's instincts had been right and that it had indeed been Seamus Quinn. Looking back over her life in New York, Hanna could never forget the debt of gratitude that she owed Maura and Andrew Jefferson. The success of her business was entirely due to the financial help that Andrew Jefferson had given her twenty-two years earlier. She remembered how in the early days of Maura's romance with the tall, handsome shipping-tycoon, she had felt the stab of sheer primitive jealousy. Maura and Andrew were without a doubt her best friends in this big, crowded adopted city and she wanted more than anything to help dispel Maura's dark ghosts, ghosts that went back to her growing years in Ireland. Her eyes left the sidewalk and swung to the buildings across the street. A brief smile crossed her face and a feeling of pride seized her, as her glance took in the Quinn-Loughlin fashion store. It was when her gaze moved to the high building on the next block and the neon light advertising *The New York Times* that an idea came to her.

Crossing the street, she walked into the high building

and took the elevator to the 10th floor. "Is Joel about?" she asked the receptionist behind the desk.

"Who will I say wants him?" she asked, picking up the telephone.

"Hanna McLaughlin," she replied with a smile.

"Are you the owner of Quinn Loughlin?"

"That's right, although I'm only a partner."

The girl smiled, "I was just looking at the winter fashion window display at lunch-time. I loved the coats and hats."

"Thank you. Why don't you come in and have a look around sometime?"

"Tell Joel that Hanna McLaughlin is here to see him."

Joel Millen appeared from a side door, "Well Hanna, this is a surprise." Smiling, he ushered her to a chair in his office. Sitting down opposite him, Hanna took in his dark bold features and as a smile crossed his face, he seemed strikingly handsome. She had known Joel for the best part of ten years and he had asked her out on numerous occasions since the death of her husband. She had always refused. Going out with another man would seem like a betrayal as far as Hanna was concerned and anyway, there was only one love in her life, she had told Joel.

"To what do I owe this unexpected pleasure?"

"I need a … a favour. There was a fatality outside the Central Bank two days ago. Would you happen to know the name of the man that was killed?"

"I do. But can't tell you yet; relatives have to be

informed first. That's the rules."

"Bend them a bit - just for me," she said, with an appealing smile of encouragement. "No can do. I'd like to help you Hanna, you know that, but rules are rules."

He looked at her longingly, noting her silky black hair, dark blue eyes and a complexion that was white and soft as doeskin. In the immaculate blue suit she looked the picture of elegance. "Why do you want to know his name?" he asked.

Hanna sighed deeply before she answered. "It's complicated. A very good friend of mine thought she recognised him and I want to set her mind at rest. If you tell me - it will go no further, I promise. Please," she added.

The pleading smile she gave him, the faint whiff of her perfume and vulnerable beauty were working on him like whiskey on a cold day, blunting the edge of his caution.

"If you agree to let me take you out to dinner one evening I … I might consider it," he said with a half smile.

"That's blackmail. But all right - it's a deal."

Going over to a desk he picked up a pile of loose sheets of paper and returned to where she sat. "This is totally unorthodox," he reminded her.

"I won't breathe a word," Hanna said, her suspension mounting.

"Let's see. Seamus Quinn was his name, and you

didn't hear this from me remember."

Hanna sat in silence for a while, letting the information sink home, "My God, she was right," she half whispered.

"Am I allowed to know why this old guy was so important; important enough to risk having dinner with the likes of me for example?" he asked with a quizzical expression.

"It's too complicated to explain right now. All I'll say is it is good news for my friend." Getting up she went towards the door, then stopped and looked back at Joel. "I'm glad I agreed to have dinner with you," she said, a smile lighting up her face. "It will have to be tomorrow mind you. I have someone I must go to see this evening."

"The name?" She nodded.

"Remember what I said. My head's on the block if you breathe a word," he called after her.

"I know. You can rely on me," she answered from the door.

Getting out of the elevator, she made for the exit door a feeling of elation enveloping her. Crossing the city to her apartment, she enjoyed the warm, autumn sun on her face and a sense of excitement generated by the hurrying crowds and noisy traffic. She felt absorbed in the millions of lives that were flowing around her, pleasantly sustained by the limitless promise of the big city. Then she thought of the deep contrast of her early life in rural Ireland, the townland, the name for every rock, every field, the narrow grey roads that wound around the hills, the strict moral code of the church and the intimate knowledge of one another. How strange then, that mere fate should have touched the lives of Maura and Seamus Quinn, thousands of miles away from Ireland.

When she reached her apartment, she flung off her jacket, picked up the telephone and called Maura. As she waited for an answer, Hanna decided not to tell her over the telephone and instead arranged to meet her at her home in half an hour. Replacing the phone in the cradle, she rushed out again and hailed a cab. Maura had coffee and cookies ready when she arrived. They sat down at the table close to the window overlooking the garden.

"What's so urgent that brings you back so soon?" Maura enquired.

"I found out something about the other day. You know … the bank."

Maura looked at her with round fearful eyes as a sickening fear took hold of her. She swallowed hard, "Out with it. Tell me what you … you found out."

"It was him and he's dead. He's dead Maura. Gone for good and all - out of your life and everyone else's." Maura began to visibly shake as the information slowly sunk into her consciousness. "Are you sure? Are you sure?" She repeated, her eyes searching Hanna's. "Couldn't be more sure. I found out at the bank that the man involved in the accident had died on his way to hospital. But nobody knew his name. Then when I saw *The Time*s office I knew Joel would know and so I went and asked him. At first he refused to tell me - relatives to be informed, he said.

Anyway I got it out of him in the end - at a price."

"And there was you saying I imagined it, million to one chance you said. But I knew even though I told myself I was imagining things again."

They looked at each other in silence for a while before Hanna spoke again. "Maura, this means that you are free from that fear of him. He can never hurt you again and you can honestly tell your daughter that her father is dead.

I believe it's fate. If I hadn't been held up at that fashion show, you might never have known."

Maura's gaze took on a look of uncertainty again, "You said something about next of kin. Does that mean they will contact someone back in Clougher? My mother and Mary Kate are the only people who might qualify as related to him."

"Well - so what? Your mother can just write back and tell them she is no relation of his."

"Let them bury him here. Cremate him, that's the best thing," she added with a nod of satisfaction. Write to your mother and tell her what's happened and then go out and celebrate."

"He may be dead Hanna … but his memory will not be so easily wiped out."

Hanna's voice took on a softer tone, "I know Maura. But you mustn't let him spoil all that you have. Andrew, the boys, Mary Kate, your business success - everything you have strived for. If you keep his bad memory alive, he will have won even in death. We have come a long way Maura. You have come a long way in spite of everything and don't you forget it."

A broad smile suddenly lit up Maura's face, "We've come a long way all right. You are scarcely recognisable as the raw young girl that shared my cabin. Remember the storm?" Hanna nodded.

"I can still hear your loud praying and see your Rosary Beads dangling down close to my face in the bunk below me. As for me, I didn't care if I lived or died at that time. You're right. We have come a long way, you and me."

Hanna smiled and got to her feet, "I'd better be going. Have you told Andrew yet?"

"No, but I will this evening. We are going up to the mountains for the weekend to join the boys."

Turning around from the doorway, Hanna said, "I was once really jealous of you - I suppose in a way I still am."

"What? Explain yourself!" Maura demanded, with a puzzled expression.

"I was jealous of you having Andrew. God, I thought he was the most gorgeous man on legs. Don't look so startled, it was only a passing phase."

"Go on, away you go before we fall out," Maura

laughed. "And by the way, what price did you have to pay Joel for the information?"

"Go out to dinner with him."

Maura laughed. "That's the best deal I ever heard of. He's a nice man Hanna and you have been on your own far too long."

"I suppose. If I wait for the magic of another Daniel, I'll be waiting forever."

When she had gone, Maura sat quietly staring at the dead leaves spiralling in the wind, trying to get her thoughts together. Later she became aware of Andrew's footsteps echoing in the hallway, "Maura, are you home?" he called.

"I'm here," she called back. "Didn't realise it was that time already."

Going into the kitchen, she busied herself getting dinner ready. Later when they had eaten, they sat opposite each other in silence for a while.

"Going to tell me what's up?" he asked with eyebrows raised.

"I can't have any secrets from you. You read me like a book," she commented, before going on to tell him the events of the past few days.

"Why didn't you tell me this before?" he asked.

"Because I wanted to face my fear and because you have had your share of misery because of my past ghosts," she ended in a sigh.

Getting up, he walked over to where she sat. He moved with a boyish smoothness and certainty that was surprising in a man so tall. Taking both her hands in his, he pulled her to a standing position. Putting a hand under her chin, he lifted her head. "Maura you should have told me all this," he said hoarsely, locking her in his arms. She pulled him closer, burying her face in his jacket.

"I wanted to face up to my own fears for once," she answered, breaking away and looking up into his face. The tone was casual, but Maura's eyes glowed like the blue centre of a candle flame. "I love you," she said simply.

"Maura I'm so proud of you. I'm more proud of you than you will ever know. And now we can go to your mother's wedding in peace."

Chapter 19

Reflections

Late summer melted into autumn; mellow light came to the hills, a cooler wind blew in from the sea sending the leaves swirling from the trees. In the orchard Sara Quinn saw the ripe apples fall to the ground, whipped from their branches by the wind. She could see the windows of the old house rising above the trees, and her thoughts went back to the first time she had come to live here as a sixteen-year-old on her first paid employment. Remembering the harsh treatment meted out to her by the Rector's wife, made her shudder. Was it to escape her and the hard grinding work that had made her decide to rush into marriage with John Quinn, she asked herself? She remembered now when he proposed to her on a Sunday afternoon as they strolled behind the grey-stone wall of the garden close to where she was standing now.

"It's hard managing on my own since my mother went," he had begun. "The place is in sore need of a woman's touch." She had stared at him, fascinated, as he passed a long tuft of heather to and fro between his fingers.

"I could fix the house up a bit - do a few repairs and that," he went on. It was only when they neared the back door of the Rectory that he asked her, "Will you take me Sara?"

Startled by the suddenness of his proposal, she looked away for a while and when she looked back at him, his shoulders had shrugged forward, his lips pouted, "Don't turn me down Sara. You will want for nothing. I have a brave bit of land and I'll work hard for you." He looked lost and appealing in the half-light and as her thoughts went back to the daily drudgery at the Rectory she said, "All right. I'll take you."

"Right then. Good. Now we need to set a date."

And so at seventeen she had walked down the isle with John Quinn to a life of hard work on a farm of stubborn, hilly ground. And yet, she had been happy enough with her lot for the most part and she had been no stranger to hard work. She slotted into the role of homemaker and mother with ease. John had, at first, been kind enough to her, even though he expected her to take over the role that his mother had left vacant, a role of cooking, cleaning and general farmhand. It was only when Maura's pregnancy and the awful circumstances surrounding it happened that her life became a living nightmare and she had been forced to leave him. She remembered the pain of parting with her only daughter now, as acutely as if it were yesterday. She felt Maura's hand, ice cold, grasp hers. She felt the quick catch of her breath as they stood at the dock on the day of their parting. Yet out of this had come Mary Kate, and James Thompson and the true friendship of Molly and James's aunt Jean.

She made her way down the steep slope and sat on the flat heathery hill overlooking the sea. She had often escaped the house to this spot over the years when the need for solitude was overwhelming.

It became increasingly evident to Sara that Mary Kate's feelings for the stranger Colin Phillips, were becoming serious and this knowledge disturbed her.

The need to talk to an old friend had been on her mind for days and so she left the hillside and walked along the coast road to visit Eleanor.

Sara sat in Eleanor's warm kitchen sipping tea from a china cup. The two women sat for a while in a comfortable silence before Sara said with a sigh, "Mary Kate has a new man in her life. His name is

Secrets on the Breeze

Colin Phillips - you know, the fellow that was engaged to the Fleming girl from Clougher Hill?"

"I get the impression that you aren't pleased."

"Oh … he seems nice enough. She brought him in to say hello before they went to the pictures one evening. But he has a … a past. They say he wanders the hills since the girl was killed or committed suicide - or whatever happened the poor soul. It's just that a man grieving and on the rebound could spell trouble."

Eleanor busied herself at the stove, pouring boiling water into the tea-pot, "A wee fresh cup," she said, as she poured more tea before sitting down again.

"So you're worried about Mary Kate and the new man in her life. Well, I'd say Mary Kate is a fairly good judge of people. She soon gave that Mike short shift when she found out his true nature. No I wouldn't worry about her judgement Sara, if I were you. She's no fool. And as for Colin Phillips - I think I'd fall for him myself, if I was young again. Something so appealing and mysterious about him."

"How do you know him?"

"Oh, I went to the girl's funeral way back. And then he came here one day to see me - sort of to thank me I suppose. I taught the wee girl for a while you see."

Sara looked directly at Eleanor and said quietly, "It's just that some men never seem to get over their first love. I'm thinking of James Thompson and all his wasted years, years of grieving and guilt with only the bottle for consolation.

And then there's Clougher itself - the place I mean. She went there you know and even visited the old house - his old house. She told me she had an eerie feeling about the place . My stomach turned over. I tried not to let it show mind you. But I hate the very mention of the place."

Eleanor looked at her friend in silence for a while and then she said, "Sara, you are creating obstacles in your head. Mary Kate is no fool. She won't sell her hen on a rainy day. I watched her handle one fellow she thought she fell for. She soon got him out of her hair, when she found out that he was a philanderer. Oh, she was hurt by him I'll grant you, but she kept that well hidden. No - I would let her get on with this new man in her life. She'll soon know if he's right for her or not. And as for that other business of Seamus Quinn, well, I'd just put it away into the back of your mind. He will probably never be seen or heard of again. We worry far too much about what might happen - far too much."

"I hope he's dead," Sara said. "Oh God, doesn't that sound awful? But I hope he's dead and done with it," she added with a nod of her head. "I believe in hell. But if you were to ask me if anyone was in hell - well, I might give you an argument. Who am I to put a limit on God's mercy?"

"Do you think he's dead?" Eleanor asked.

She shook her head, "I don't know. The last I heard of him was from that young woman Jean McGreggor in Canada. He was apparently in bad shape the last time she set eyes on him. She said she'd let me know if she heard anything more. But she was leaving that mining place before her baby was born. The worst of it is, that the police found out that he has money in a New York bank and I'm fearful that if he mended up a bit he might make for there to get hold of it."

"You are letting your imagination run amok Sara and that's not like you."

"Oh, I suppose you're right. But when it comes to him I'm - I'm not rational. So much heartbreak in my life was caused by him, so much sorrow. If only someone had had the courage to get rid of him long ago."

"Easier said than done Sara - secrets, secrets, secrets. Sometimes I think my whole life has been made up of them. Sometimes in my minds eye, I see my mother in that hateful house, the colour drained from her face and her eyes bright with desperation and fear, because she had a secret that had to be kept. What a waste of a life. What a shameful waste. And I didn't get off scott-free either. There was a price for me to pay too. I blamed myself - if it hadn't been for me she wouldn't have married the brute. Because I had to keep this secret too, I swung the door of those precious childhood years shut on the bright, menacing world."

"Enough of this Sara. What about your wedding outfit? Did you get it yet?"

"Aye."

"Well - well what's it like?"

"It's a sort of ivory taffeta. Far too grand for me, after all it's only a convenience thing. But Maura and Mary Kate insisted I look the part."

"And so you should Sara. Make it special. You are two very special people and you deserve to have a special day and to be happy."

"There's no romance in it. It's just James' idea for giving that wee girl a home."

"Ah, come on Sara, what's wrong with a bit of romance? And James Thompson is a bit of a catch. He's a very distinguished looking man and a talented one to boot."

"Go on with you. I told you - it's only a marriage of convenience. Let's get out for a walk in the sun," she said, standing up and smoothing down her skirt.

They walked in silence along the shore, each lost in their own thoughts as they watched the seaweed-carts making their laborious way inland along the narrow track. To the casual observer, they were two respectably dressed, middle-aged women out for a stroll. Who could have guessed the secret fears from old and bitter wounds that still haunted them.

Chapter 20

The Meeting

Mary Kate walked between the big pillars and along the dark avenue with slow uncertain steps. When the big stone building came into view she stopped and stared at the sheer bulk of the grey stone walls and thought of Rebecca. In that moment a fearful panic came over her and she had to stop herself from fleeing.

The desperation that drove her here began to subside in her moment of panic.

Colin had promised to be with her on Friday evening and she had waited all evening for him. After a disturbed night's sleep and a day spent waiting by the window, she could bear it no longer and now she stood facing the big house with its fearful shadows. She stared at the rising moon, remote and unfeeling. "Lucky moon, what do you know of love?" she whispered.

Three weeks had passed since she last saw Colin. Had he forgotten her? And she, for her part had tried and failed to throw him out of her heart and mind.

She ventured forward up the stone steps. A bright light shone from the hallway as her trembling hand pulled the doorbell cord, sending echoes into the distance. The wind held its breath as it sometimes did and in the silence her heart said "Please God, let Colin be here. Let him be safe - let him still care."

The door suddenly swung open, revealing a middle-aged woman wearing a white apron. Mary Kate licked her dry lips, "Is Colin Phillips … here?"

The woman shook her head, "He hasn't come this weekend."

"Could I come in and have a word with Mr Fleming then?"

The woman's face darkened, "Who are you?"

"I'm Mary Kate Quinn. Mr Phillips knows … knows of me. I just need to ask him something. Please just for a minute?"

"Wait here and I'll see what he says." Mary Kate waited with a thundering heart. One, two chimed the grandfather clock, "Please God, let him be all right," she whispered as she waited.

Secrets on the Breeze

The woman came back, "He'll see you. Follow me," she said, her footsteps echoing on the marble floor of the great hall. She opened a door to the left, "In here." Mary Kate followed and saw the old man seated in a wheelchair, close to a blazing fire. "This is the girl that wants to see you. Miss…."

"Mary Kate Quinn," Maura filled in for her.

She went over to where he sat, bent down and shook his hand. "I'm glad to meet you Mr Fleming."

"Sit down close to me - so I can see you. I'm glad you came because I have something to tell you."

"Is it Colin?" she almost whispered, her heart pounding.

"It's all right Martha. You can leave us now," he said, glancing towards the woman in the doorway. She seemed reluctant to leave, and as Mary Kate glanced in her direction, the hostility in her eyes was unmistakable. Finally she left them alone, closing the door behind her.

"Is Colin all right?" she asked again.

"He is. I was about to send somebody to you with a message when Martha told me you were here. Colin's mother rang me to say he had been very sick. They weren't sure what it was at first. Then some doctor at the infirmary diagnosed it as Typhoid Fever. Poor Colin, he had a close call. But his mother says he's over the worst."

Relief flooded through her and her body felt limp as his words sunk into her consciousness.

"Thank God. Thank you God," she repeated.

The old man studied her in silence for a while before he spoke, "You really are sweet on him. He told me all about you a few weeks ago."

Meeting his gaze, Mary Kate felt herself flush. "I'm sorry. I must seem like an awful fool barging in here like this. I … I was just so anxious when he didn't turn up."

He looked at her furtively for a moment, "I'm glad you came. Like I said, Colin has told me about you. He wanted me to be the first to know that he had asked you out. Silly that. But I suppose he thought that because of … of Rebecca," he ended lamely.

"He told me about Rebecca. I'm sorry," she added quietly.

"Let's not dwell on sad things - at least not for today."

"You are a beautiful woman. Hope you don't mind me saying so."

She blushed again, "No. No I'm flattered."

"It's a lovely house and so big," she said, glancing around the room.

He sighed deeply before he answered, "It is a fine house as far as houses go. But for me it has become a prison of loneliness - apart from when Colin's here."

She stared into the fire, unsure of how she should respond. Then she asked, "Would you like me to visit you from time to time?"

"That's very kind of you. But I don't want you to go wasting your time on an old man like me."

"It would be a pleasure and I'd like to get to know you better."

He eyed her closely again and the abruptness of his next question startled her.

"Are you in love with Colin Phillips?"

She became flustered by the abruptness of his question, "I … I only met Colin for the first time this summer. I'm … very fond of him."

"That's not what I asked. Are you in love with him?"

"He's so handsome, so heart-breaking, he's so - he made me sad and happy ..." Her voice broke a little and he knew there were tears in her throat.

When he spoke again his voice was softer, kinder, "I'm sorry if I seem so abrupt. But when you get to my age you have no time to beat about the bush. And Colin means a lot to me. I don't want to see him hurt. There are things he witnessed during the war, awful things that he can't talk about. Then there was Rebecca," he ended in a sigh. "I'm just looking out for him."

"Yes … I … I do love him. And I'm not the flighty type, if that's what you're trying to say." The thought that he knew about her past came briefly into her thoughts. "I'm not going to let my past get in the way. Never again," she vowed silently.

The anger in her tone left the old man feeling uncomfortable.

"Sorry Mary Kate. I think I've put paid to any sympathy you might have felt for me. I'm sorry. I had no right."

They sat silently staring into the fire, each lost in their own thoughts. Joe's thoughts were on Rebecca and the love he felt for her, a love that drowned out the voice that told him all was not well. He recalled nights when the southeast winds rattled the windows and he would tiptoe into the room where she slept. If her bed happened to be empty he would peer out into the night with anxious, sleepless eyes. Yet he hadn't warned Colin. Was it because he wanted her happiness so much that it had blinded him to the risks? He sighed long and deep before looking at Mary Kate again.

"I think Colin will do very well if he wins your heart Mary Kate. And if you never set foot inside my door again I … I couldn't say I'd blame you."

Getting to her feet she said, "I better be on my way. Thanks for giving me the good news."

She looked down at him and the sadness she saw in his eyes evaporated the earlier hostility she had felt towards him. Bending down she took both his hands in hers and squeezed them gently, "I'll be back," she said quietly.

"Won't you stay and have some tea?"

"Thanks, but no. I've got to get back before they send out a search party."

She let herself out through the big hall door and went out into the moonlight. She ran out into the wind as she had often done as a child, her hair streaming behind her. The dry leaves of autumn whirled out of the oaks and flew past her like a cloud of tiny migrant birds, but the leaves were dead, finished. They would not return like the birds. "Colin, please return to me. Please," she called out above the howl of the wind. At the big gates she turned her back on the wind. The old familiar stab of pain and disappointment went through her briefly, but it was replaced by the memory of Colin's kisses on their last meeting. "I'm going home to write to you Colin. And I will wait - I will wait, no matter how long it takes."

The pink flush of dawn stole over the hills as Mary Kate cycled along the lane on her way to school, her thoughts on Colin. Three weeks had past with no answer to her letter. With Christmas just a few weeks away, she found escapism in her work and tried to concentrate solely on her pupils and at their preparations for the festive season. But to escape from the storm in her own heart was not as easy as she had hoped. Why hadn't he replied to her letter? Had she been mistaken about his feelings for her? Had he recovered from his illness? Questions, questions ran around in her head, but no answers came to her. Each day on her return from school, she would dare to hope for a letter, only to be disappointed again. She tried to keep the turmoil she was feeling in her heart from Sara and James, but she knew from their anxious glances that she wasn't succeeding.

There was a Christmas tree in the drawing-room bright with tinsel and bobbles and she tried to share in the delight that her grandmother and James took in the Christmas preparations. There were many things she would like to tell these two kind, loving people with their kind, understanding eyes. Sometimes her secrets weighed heavily and it seemed to her that the fraying net of her heart was wearing too thin to keep up the pretence of being happy.

The classroom was quieter than usual, the children's heads bent in their respective tasks. "Please Miss, is this all right?" Looking down at the front row, she watched the glow of pride on wee Mary's face as she held up the Christmas card she had just finished colouring.

"That is lovely Mary. Well done."

A knock on the classroom door interrupted the class. "A letter for you Miss Quinn," a voice called from the other side of the door. When she opened the door she saw a small, middle-aged man standing there with a letter in his hand.

"Joe from the Big House sent you this," he said, and was gone. Glancing at the envelope she read; 'This came from Colin.'

She ripped open the letter and read, *'I will be with you for Christmas. Love Colin.'* Turning the sheet of paper over and over, she searched in vain for another letter, anything that would tell her how he was or how he felt. But there was nothing more than these brief few words.

Chapter 21

Sara's News

Sara saw the postman making his way across the yard, the sleety wind blowing out the tails of his long coat like dark kites. She went down the chilly hall to the back door to meet him. "There's hot tea on the range. You look like you could do with it," she said, ushering him in through the door.

When tea was over, he opened the big canvas postbag and handed her a small bundle of letters and Christmas cards. Maura's handwriting caught her eye and she opened her letter first. A quick scan of the first page told the news that she had waited for, hoped for and yet it shocked her. "He is dead. He is dead," she repeated silently.

"Not bad news?" the postman was asking her, his voice seeming to come from a great distance."

"No. No, not bad news," she found herself saying.

She was relieved when he finally went on his way and she was alone with her thoughts. She read and reread Maura's letter just to make sure that she had read it correctly the first time. "Seamus Quinn is dead. Dead. Dead, dead. Gone from our midst," she repeated again and again.

When James Thompson suddenly materialised beside her, she nearly cried out in fright. In one hand he carried a bunch of holly and in the other a brown parcel. "Are you all right Sara?" he asked, scrutinising her closely.

"My nerves are a bit on edge. Here, read this," she said, handing him the letter.

As she looked up at him, sleety snow dripping from his coat, memory jumped back to the evening long ago, when he suddenly appeared following months of absence. The scene was the same - the fire in the hearth, the darkening advance of an already gloomy day and the sound of the wind and sleet on the windows.

He looked at her and smiled, "This is good news. All things considered, it's good news," he said, sitting down on the nearest chair, the letter still in his hand. "I must go and tell Grace. I will be able to tell Mary

Kate in all truthfulness, that her father is dead."

Reaching across, he took Sara's hands in his, "Sara I'm relieved. To hell with it … I'm more than relieved. A great burden has been lifted from you … from us and if I was still a whiskey drinking man, I'd get us both a glass."

"Oh James, it seems awful to be rejoicing in somebody's death. I feel like a Ghoul."

"No. No Sara, you have nothing to reproach yourself for and you have every reason to be relieved that he's gone. You have had to keep this secret for twenty odd years. A secret that cost you far too much; took too much of your precious days worrying about. You done nothing wrong, for God's sake. Maura done no wrong. Mary Kate done no wrong and yet you all paid a heavy price for evil done to you. So unfair, so totally unfair. Sara, there will come a time in the not too distant future when the Seamus Quinn's of this world will be brought to justice. When the innocent victims will have the courage to tell their story in a court of law and be confident that justice will be done. God speed that day … is all I can say. No more whispered secrets."

As she looked into his kind eyes, she knew that the pain in her was dying now, she knew that they had come a long way and achieved much together.

"There's another letter," James said, pulling out a second letter from the envelope.

Sara read it in silence, folded it and handed it to James.

"She wants to buy a motor car for Mary Kate. A motor car, if you please."

"And why not Sara? It would be great for all of us. You know, we'd get out and about. I might even learn to drive it myself."

"Well, I suppose we must go with the times," she said, her face relaxing into an expressive smile and she put out her hand. James seized the cold bony fingers and pressed them to his lips. "Won't we all look grand driving around in the motor?" he said with a twinkle in his eyes.

Sara's face darkened again, "What if they think we're the next of kin? What will I tell Mary Kate?"

"Just put them straight and as for Mary Kate, he is just a distant cousin of her grandfather."

She smiled, "I'm a nuisance to you. A nuisance."

"Never that Sara. We still have a lot to look forward to you and me. Aye, in spite of everything we're still here."

"And it looks like we're getting a motor car," Sara added again, getting to her feet.

A pale sun had struggled through the clouds and was making a feeble effort to guild the day, Sara, feeling cold after the warmth of the train, knocked on Grace Murphy's door. When Grace answered her knock, she looked startled by the suddenness of her old neighbour's appearance on her doorstep. "It's all right Grace. No bad news," she reassured her, putting a hand briefly on Grace's shoulder. "Is the coast clear?"

"Aye, aye. I'm on my own. Come in, come in," she repeated, standing aside to let Sara in.

When they were seated, Sara handed her the letter. "Read this and then burn it," she said.

Grace bent closer to read the letter, her eyebrows performing *a pas de deux* on her forehead. When she had finished reading, she looked at Sara in silence for a moment, searching for words.

"He's dead. May the saints be praised. When I saw you on the doorstep Sara, I thought the worst."

"It's over Grace. He won't be coming back."

"Wasn't it amazing that Maura should be the one to see him killed. All the millions of people in that big city and on a million to one chance, she … she happened to be there. I call that fate. Aye - more than fate. Justice - that's what it was."

Sara nodded vigorously, "I didn't think of it like that before. But you know, you're right. The wheels of God grind exceedingly slow ..."

The two women sat close to the smouldering fire, each deep in their separate thoughts, with only the loud ticking of the clock disturbing the silence.

Sara and Grace walked slowly up the lane against the dark shoulders of the hills towards Seamus Quinn's cottage. The new slates of the roof glinted with the wetness of recent rain. Sara stopped and stared at the outline of the house, she promised herself never to see again. She found it extraordinary - his capacity for causing fear, hate and suffering - this man whose manner at one time had seemed so gentle and whose speech had always been so soft and padded. She shuddered now in remembrance of the times when he had sat at their family table and shared the food she has prepared. "Poor Seamus needs a home cooked meal. He's not much of a hand at fending for himself," John had informed her as a new bride. And so the pattern had continued until that fateful day that changed all their lives. Now, as Sara stared at the derelict house, there were no tears in her eyes, only a look of intolerable pain. As they looked at the gaping windows, two jackdaws flew in, hovered a moment in a beam of sunlight, then flew out again. They sighed deeply before walking away.

Chapter 22

Christmas

Mary Kate locked the big door of the school and
pulled the fur collar of her coat tightly around her
neck. She was glad of the Christmas break but she
could not capture the Christmas magic that she had
known in other years.

Out of the gate she walked slowly, aimlessly, away
from the school. She couldn't shake the heavy sadness
in her heart and wished that she could have stopped
herself from falling in love with a relative stranger,
who couldn't even be bothered to write her a letter.

By the time she reached the Rectory gates the light

was fading and the cold easterly wind tugged at her coat and whipped her hair into her eyes. Her thoughts went to the comfort of the warm fire and hot soup that would be waiting for her, quickening her steps. In the warm kitchen Sara and James greeted her warmly, "You look frozen love. Come and get warmed up," she said, opening the door of the range. Feeling revived from the warmth from the range fire and Sara's hot soup, James sat down at the other end of the range and lit his pipe. "I'm going to accompany you both to Midnight Mass on Christmas Eve," he announced with a grin. "In most people's terms it's no great shakes. But considering my past record on Christian observance - it's well - a bit unusual. I can just see the stares we'll get."

Mary Kate's thoughts went back to Colin. She let her imagination play on the idea of Colin and herself sitting side by side in the wee church.

It could do so much to bring them closer together, to deepen a dawning love, sitting side by side in the wee church on Christmas Eve contemplating the serious meaning of life.

She sighed deeply and stared into space. "You're not even listening to me."

"Sorry, Sorry. I was miles away." As she looked into his kind face, she could feel the tears behind her eyes coming close to the surface.

"Still no word of him?" he asked quietly. She shook her head.

"He'll turn up. I know he will."

She shook her head again, "He doesn't really care or he would have come - written, something. I've been a fool again," she added, staring into the distance.

Putting down his pipe he pulled his chair closer and put his arm around her shoulder and held her in silence. At last she made a little sound … almost a moan and pressed her face against his shoulder. "What can I do James?"

He knew a great heaviness of heart before he answered. "You will be all right Mary Kate. Whatever happens … you will be all right. And if this man is meant for you he'll come." She gave him a weak smile, "God … I'm a nuisance to you. But I won't spoil Christmas and I'll proudly sit beside you at Midnight Mass."

"That's more like it. Talking about churches and that. I can't help hearing Molly's voice in my head. She attributed my success in giving up the drink to the power of prayer. 'Your beating the drink was my prayers and the prayers I've asked the Poor Clare nuns to offer up for you,' she used to tell me. I'm not scoffing this theory. I think that prayer is a powerful thing to have working on your side."

"Are you telling me to pray that Colin will come back to me? Pray to the Saint for lost love or lost causes," she added, with a broad grin."

"You're no lost cause Mary Kate. You are the best thing that ever happened to me and to all of us. And what's more, if this Colin fellow has an ounce of common sense, he'll be back to claim you double quick."

"I wish I had such faith in me." She smiled at him and kissed him lightly on the cheek before going to her room.

In the village shops Mary Kate chose the Christmas gifts for Sara and James and tried to make an effort to capture the spirit of the season but her heart wasn't in it.

She left the village carrying her purchases as the last of the daylight lingered, as though reluctant to depart. She had meant to walk home, but an hour later she found herself at the big gates of Joe's house. Outside the railings she gazed upwards at the lights in the windows. Uncertain about what to do next, she saw the headlights of a car coming up the road. She slid behind the stone pillar as the car swung in through the gates and along the gravel path. She watched the headlamps go out and saw a darkened shadow climb the stone steps to the front door and she instinctively knew that it was Colin.

Standing up, she half ran back down the laneway, tears streaming down her face. Out of the darkness she could make out the dark outline of a barn, she found the doorway and went inside. Sitting down on a pile of straw, the countless noises of the farmyard rising all around, she tried to regain some composure.

From time to time huge shadows loomed across the far end of the barn. She sat there a long time, her mind blank "What is the point of forcing myself to think? Someone was sure to explain to me, someone who would explain everything - why Colin has abandoned me, the reason for my journey to Joseph Fleming's gates, the reason why I can't get him out of my head."

She would never be sure how long she stayed there alone with her pain, but eventually she arrived back home, cold, confused and exhausted.

Colin Phillips put down his heavy suitcases and pulled the bell. He could hear Martha Morgan's footsteps echoing from within. Martha had been with the Flemings for the best part of twenty years and her grief at Rebecca's death had not subsided. After greeting Martha at the door, he put down his suitcases and went straight to the small sitting-room. Joe lay on a sofa, propped up against a pile of pillows, a book in his hand.

His face lit up when he saw Colin. "Great to see you back. I've been waiting all evening for you. Help me up to the chair," he said, reaching out his bony hand from under the rug.

When Colin had helped him into his wheelchair, he asked, "What did Mary Kate say when you delivered my letters."

"What letters?"

Secrets on the Breeze

"I sent two letters for you to deliver. Don't you remember telling me on the phone that you wanted me to send the letters here, so you would have an excuse to go and see her? You said you wanted to make amends for the bad start - you know, when you told me you half interrogated her the night she came to see you," he added, the tone of his voice becoming agitated.

The old man looked at him with a puzzled frown, "I'm not that far gone. I waited for the letter you told me you'd send and I was waiting to go to meet her from the school. I even told John to have the motor at the ready as soon as it arrived. But nothing come and I naturally thought you'd had second thoughts - changed your mind about her."

"For God's sake Joe - I told you how I feel about her. And now I've probably lost her. I posted two letters here … here to this address. I could maybe see one going astray. But two, no, that's too fishy."

"For God's sake Colin, you're not surely accusing me of … of hiding the letters? You know me better than that surely?"

"No, Joe, no. I know you wouldn't do that. But where did they disappear to?

Do you get your letters directly from the postman?"

"No … no Martha brings them."

The old man suddenly looked troubled as his eyes moved to the door, "Martha, my God, she couldn't," he almost whispered.

"Rebecca." Joe nodded, swallowing hard. "Go and find her. You say nothing. Just tell her I want to see her."

Colin found Martha slumped in an armchair beside the kitchen stove, "Mr. Fleming wants to see you," he said, nudging her shoulder. She sat up with a start, rubbing her eyes.

"Oh. Oh, I was just dozing. Is he all right?" she asked, getting to her feet and smoothing her apron. She appeared a model of stout, complacent efficiency. Colin knew her sort. Loyal to those who hired her, grateful for the dog-to-master relationship and standing up for them against her own kind. Would that very, misguided loyalty cause her to destroy his letters, he wondered as they made their way along the dim corridor to where Joe waited.

"Martha I need to ask you something very important," Joe began, as she stood before him.

"What is it Mr Fleming?" she asked with a puzzled frown on her plump face.

"Colin sent two very important letters here addressed to Mary Kate Quinn. I told you some time back that I was waiting for them," he continued. "But I didn't get them. Can you throw any light on this?"

Her face darkened and her eyes narrowed before she spoke, "I know nothing about any letters. Must have got lost in the post. The name Quinn would … would … have thrown the postman most likely."

"No Martha. They were addressed to Mary Kate

Quinn, care of Joseph Fleming, at this very address. No, the postman is not that dim."

Her face reddened, "I know nothing about them," she said with an air of defiance.

"Martha. You took them letters because of Rebecca didn't you? Didn't you?" He repeated.

Her face, blazing with anger, she turned to Colin, "It didn't take you long to find someone else, did it? She deserved better than that. You run off with the first bit of skirt you could find. I took them letters and burned them. I burned them in the fireplace in Rebecca's room. I did it for my poor wee Rebecca."

"My God, woman don't you know what you've done. You stole personal letters, letters that belonged to someone else. I wouldn't be surprised if you didn't read them before you burned them."

"Aye, aye, I read them."

The silence that followed was only broken by the grandfather clock in the hall striking the hour.

"Please don't tell me to go Mr Fleming. I did it for my Rebecca … I did it for her," suddenly her shoulders slumped and she began to sob quietly, the fight all gone out of her. In that moment Colin's earlier anger and resentment was replaced by pity.

"Just go Martha. Just go," Joe was saying. She walked backwards towards the door, wiping her eyes with the tail of her white apron.

When she at last closed the door they sat in silence for a while before Joe said, "I'm sorry Colin so … so sorry. I pray to God that you can make amends."

"I must go to her now. I must try to explain," he said, grabbing his coat from the back of the chair.

"Wouldn't it be better to wait till the morning?"

"I can't wait that long. I must know now. I must tell her."

"I'm sorry," Joe repeated.

"It wasn't your fault. It wasn't your fault," he repeated, closing the door behind him. Joe sat in silence listening to Colin's rapid footsteps echo away and sighed deeply into the silence.

Colin drove along the dark lanes his thought running wildly around in his head. Martha destroying his letters to Mary Kate had shocked him to the core. He remembered now, hearing her voice coming from Rebecca's room in the dead of night and had dismissed it as the grief of a lonely middle-aged woman for a girl she had practically reared.

During these last weeks he had suffered a constant warring within himself as he lay in his hospital bed. He longed for Mary Kate and at times of high fever he could have sworn he heard her voice, saw her face and felt her touch.

Then, as he began to recover his thoughts went to the Donegal countryside that he had grown to love. In his mind, he could see the ice carved scenery, the stern hill peaks lathered with white frothy clouds and the flat crevices where the blue heather grew. He would walk with Mary Kate by the tiny mountain streams that trickled from the steep hillsides and he would stop to kiss her, the air silent save for the rushing stream. These were the dreams that kept his sanity.

His car headlamps lit up the grey stone of the Rectory as the car came to a halt in front of it. Getting out he closed the car door and headed for the front door, his nerves straining out into the silence. There was no sound of any kind, beyond the house or from within it as he grabbed the knocker, gave three loud knocks and waited.

Finally a light appeared from within the hallway and the door opened to reveal a middle-aged man carrying an oil lamp, peering out at him.

"I'm Colin Phillips. I've come to see Mary Kate," Colin said, trying to disguise the fear that suddenly gripped him.

James wished that Sara hadn't decided to go to Eleanor's this evening, of all evenings. He hadn't known what to do when Mary Kate came home earlier, tearful, and distraught and he had failed to discover the reason. But he suspected it had something to do with this stranger on his doorstep.

"I don't think Mary Kate will want to see you. You've caused her enough misery already. Goodnight." He made to close the door, "Please, please let me see her. Just for a minute I … I can explain. I've been sick, in the hospital.

The letters I sent her were stolen."

"Come back tomorrow. Though I doubt if she'll want

to see you," he added, making to close the door again.
A fist seemed to tighten over his heart and crush it.
"Please. I love her for God's sake," he almost shouted.
In near desperation he put his right foot inside the
door. "Please at least let me explain."

"Mary Kate's in bed. But I suppose you better come
in," he added, standing aside.

He opened a door to the right and nodded for Colin
to enter. Then pointing to an armchair he indicated
for him to sit down. He put the lamp on the table and
sat down at the opposite side of the fire.

"Mary Kate came home this evening exhausted,
frozen to the bone and confused. Were you the cause
of this?" James Thompson asked, his tone angry and
his eyes blazing.

"No. No I just arrived this evening myself and I
haven't even seen her yet.

That's why I'm here, to … to explain."

"You've been playing cat and mouse with her
affections and I want you to stay away from her. She
is my daughter in all but name. I heard her first words,
saw her take her first step and I won't have her
heartbroken by the likes of you."

As though his mind, dormant for the past weeks, had
gathered its forces, Colin experienced a burst of
power. "Please Mr Thompson, hear me out before
you pass judgment on me."

James nodded for him to begin and when he had
finished talking, there was a long silence. Then James

asked, "What about the Fleming girl? The girl that died, are … you still grieving for her?"

"I'm saddened by her death, the way she died. But if you mean, is Mary Kate second best, then the answer is no. And after the episode with Martha, the housekeeper - I made up my mind tonight - that I won't spend any more time in that house. It's a place of whispering ghosts. Mind you, I'm very fond of old Joe. He's a lonely old man. Do you think she would see me tonight? Would you ask if she could see me just for a few minutes?"

James looked at the honest face of the young man sitting before him, and realized that more than anything he wanted his approval.

"Very well. I'll go and see what she has to say."

James knocked quietly on Mary Kate's door, "Who is it?" her muffled voice came from within. "It's only me. I have something to tell you."

She opened the door slowly and even in the dim light, he could tell that she had been crying.

"Your young man is downstairs and wants to see you." She shook her head, "I won't see him. He doesn't really want me."

"Oh, but he does. We have been talking for the last hour or more and he has passed my test. Mind you - I didn't make it easy for him. But he did write you letters and he will explain everything." She stood shivering and uncertain, not taking her eyes from

Hazel McIntyre

James's face.

"Put the poor man out of his misery," he said quietly. Suddenly she smiled, "I must look a sight. Give me five minutes."

"He's in the sitting room," he said, from the door.

He stood up when she went into the room and from the corner of her eye she saw James leave, closing the door quietly behind him. They looked at each other in silence and then he walked towards her and then his hands were enclosing her own and she felt the old familiar thrill of weakness shiver through her body, and his voice, the deep beautiful voice that had attracted her so much was telling her he loved her. He caught hold of her arm and tucked her to him as they talked in quiet whispers by the dying embers of the fire.

Later they walked outside and along the gravel path. On the eastern hump of the hills, a thin silver crescent of a moon was rising in the cold star-frosted sky. Arms around each other, they stood in silence, listening to the night - the waves crashing against the rocks below and the breeze in the dark hills behind them.

From the kitchen window James and Sara stood silently watching their silhouette against the night sky.

"Well James, it looks as if our wee girl has found what she was searching for."

"Aye Sara. I think she has."

Sara sighed softly, "Maybe he will take her away to

Scotland with him."

"Nope."

"How do you know?"

"Well - I sort of enquired."

"You mean you interrogated him?" She could hear him chuckle softly and then she felt his arm go around her shoulder. Putting her own arm around his waist, she said, "You are a wonder James. We have travelled some road together you and me."

"And there is still a bit of ground to cover."

Sara smiled, "Aye James, Aye."

Chapter 23

The Party 1976

Sara smoothed her thinning grey hair neatly under the net and sat stiffly down on the chair beside her bedroom window, looking out across the familiar scene of sea and hill. She suddenly remembered that it was her birthday, "I am old, I am very old" she thought. On the distant hillside she could see sheep grazing in the spring sunshine and down below in the garden, she watched young Kate, a tall young woman, who looked the image of her father, pegging washing on the line. My great granddaughter, she whispered with a thin smile. The long past began to flow through her like an ebb tide bearing away its treasures. Images once loved and treasured rose and faded. James - her lips formed his name, James, who was gone these past twelve years, James my darling you are near me now. "We shared so much - joys, and sorrows and whispered secrets." Memories of all the people she had known and loved came back to her now - her mother, old Molly, Jean, Eleanor … "gone, all gone and I'm still spared" she whispered into the silence. Warmed by the spring sunshine, she lay back in the chair and listened to the uneven beat of her weary old heart and fell into a doze.

"Granny, I brought you some tea," Mary Kate's voice woke her.

"Oh, I was having a wee doze."

"Happy birthday granny," she said, planting a kiss on her forehead.

"So you didn't forget."

"As if? We are having a wee celebration for you a bit later on."

"That's thoughtful of you Mary Kate. You always were thoughtful and … and you have a kind heart. Worth a-rearing, as my mother would have said."

"What about Colin? Is he back from Scotland yet?"

"He'll be back in a while. You know he wouldn't miss your big day for anything."

"He's a grand fellow is Colin. You've been lucky in him Mary Kate.

Mind you I had my doubts in the beginning. But James put my mind at rest on that score. Aye, he was a good judge of people was James. I still miss him you know."

"So do I granny. I'll always miss him. He was the only father I'd ever known and what good fortune I had in him and in you."

"Thanks darling," she said, catching her hand briefly and squeezing it.

In the kitchen Maura was putting the last touches to the birthday cake, "Well, how is she?" she asked, glancing briefly at her daughter.

"She seems in good enough form."

"Does she suspect anything do you think?"

Mary Kate shook her head, "She seemed surprised that I even remembered it was her birthday. I hope the shock of seeing you doesn't give her a heart attack. She still lives in the age of steam trains and steamships. Air travel all the way from America, wouldn't be part of her thinking.

And tell Andrew to keep well out of her line of vision, for she has eyes like a hawk, ninety or not. She doesn't miss a thing that passes that window."

"Right I'll warn him," she said, leaving the kitchen by the side door.

Alone, Mary Kate sighed as she thought about the strangeness of having a mother, stepfather and half-brothers she barely knew. They had inhabited two separate worlds and it was something she couldn't change.

Secrets on the Breeze

Later as they sat at either end of the table buttering the bread for sandwiches, Maura, lost in her own thoughts was unprepared for the question her daughter sprung on her.

"Mother - you have never really told me who I am. Who my father was."

"Who you are?" She glanced up, startled. And an old childhood fear gripped her heart. "Why … why … are you asking me this now?"

Mary Kate leaned forward and her gaze rested on Maura with a queer searching expression that was part resentful and part affectionate.

"Don't you think I have the right to know?"

"I am your mother and I love you. All right, I wasn't the mother to you that I wanted to be and I've told you why. A young unmarried girl giving birth to a baby back then was treated like a criminal."

"I know all that. But you haven't answered my question."

Maura's gaze went to the window and after sighing deeply her gaze went back to Mary Kate.

"His name was John. John Quinn, a second cousin of mine. I was young, and foolish and ignorant and he took advantage of that. He's dead now. Died in the States long ago. There is nothing more to tell you about him Mary Kate.

I'm sorry I've been less of a mother than I'd like to have been. When I first knew that I was going to have a baby I - I was devastated, panic stricken. Then when your grandfather found out he packed me off to the nuns - a just pack your bags and get out of my sight - save the family's good name at all costs. Well, It was hell. I was alone and terrified. Then you were born and they let me hold you and I thought you were the most perfect and beautiful wee being in the planet. I hadn't bargained for that," she said, tears now beginning to mist her eyes. She sighed and looked away from Mary Kate, then she said, "One morning they took you away and I could hear you crying somewhere in the distance, but I couldn't find you and I was desperate - desperate.

Two days later I was put on a ship bound for New York. No warning, no nothing."

"I'm sorry," Mary Kate said quietly. "All the bother and trouble I caused."

"Oh God, Mary Kate - please don't say that. You were the innocent one and I'm not telling you all this because I want pity. I'm just trying to make you understand," she added looking into the deep-set soulful eyes of her daughter, so much like her own.

"I came back here when you were about two and a half. I had this grand notion of moving into the old home-place with you and we would live happily ever after. Well, we left here you and me - and it was only then that I knew - you were more your grandmother's and James Thompson's child than my own.

You cried to go home, stopped eating and sleeping. I had to take you back here - I had no other option."

Secrets on the Breeze

Her gaze went back to the window again and then she said, as if to herself, "I will never forget how you ran into their arms when we got here. The joy on your wee face and the joy in their faces told me I had failed. But I was jealous of them. I was so jealous that I sulked in my room like a wee baby and cried into my pillow night after night."

As Mary Kate looked at the tear-stained face of her mother and saw the pain in her eyes, the beginnings of understanding her, for the first time began to seep into her consciousness. A silence followed before Mary Kate her voice calm and reflective said, "There were times when I almost hated you. I had you down as a mother who thought that gifts of fancy clothes and money made up for abandoning me. When I was a wee girl in school, I was the odd one out. 'You have no mammy and daddy,' they would sneer. And, God, how I hated it. I would show them photos of this handsome couple with their two wee boys, dressed to kill, and tell them that was my mammy, and daddy and wee brothers. But if you were to ask me if I'd have been better off with you in New York, my answer would be no. Granny and James were the best parents any child could have wished for. And then there was old Jean and Molly. They fussed over me like a pair of clocking hens with one chick. Nobody will ever know how much I grieved when James Thompson died." "I grieved for him too Mary Kate, maybe I wasn't as close to him as you. But I owed him so much. If it hadn't been for him, Andrew and me wouldn't have had our life together."

Mary Kate looked at her mother with a quizzical frown, "He went all the way to New York to see Andrew for me. I met Andrew when I was a nanny to his brother's child and then when we fell in love, I couldn't tell him about my past. Fear of rejection I suppose, so ... so I ran away. Well, I was back here and you didn't need me - not in the way I wanted to be needed." She looked away before continuing, the words were coming faster as if she had to tell everything, as if time were running out. "Anyway," she went on, "I confided in James Thompson and he went to New York without telling me, saw Andrew, explained my sudden departure and the rest is history."

"Andrew and me wanted to take you back to New York with us. But it would have broken their hearts. And young as you were, I knew you didn't want to leave them either. So Mary Kate, that's about it."

Mary Kate made an effort to smile "I'm glad you told me all this. It's helped to get things a bit clearer in my mind."

"Your grandmother was the hero in all this really. She sacrificed a lot for us. She made me a promise on the dockside on the day I was transported to America, when she promised to take you out of the orphanage and look after you until I got back. She had to lie to the nuns to get you out. And when she came here it was to a dilapidated, run-down ramshackle of a house.

But she transformed the lives of everyone under this roof and made the place habitable again. Then there was the gossips of this wee community. A woman back then walking out on her man and living under another's roof was a disgrace. She was even taken to task by the Parish Priest."

Mary Kate sighed and then a puzzled look came into her eyes before she asked, "What do you mean by lie to the nuns to get me out?"

Maura sighed, as if struggling for the right words to explain, "Women had no rights back in the twenties. And when the man of the house gave orders they were obeyed. My father, your grandfather, gave instructions to the nuns that I was to be put on a liner for New York and that you were to be brought up in the orphanage. So your grandmother had to lie and tell them he'd changed his mind. If they hadn't believed her, his word would have been law."

"Bastard. Cruel Bastard."

"He was a part of his own time - the strict moral code - and if it's any comfort Mary Kate, he lived long enough to regret his stubborn cruelty. He wasn't a bad man, as bad men go. I still have the letter he wrote me begging forgiveness and I reasoned that if your grandmother could forgive him, then I could too."

"Did she never tell you this?" Mara Kate shook her head, "But I think I have a vague memory of him in the kitchen here and in the old nursery upstairs. I was frightened of him if memory serves me right."

"He told me in the letter about seeing you and how you reminded him of me at that age. Your grandmother took him in when he was nearing the end. He died in this house."

"When it comes to granny, nothing would surprise me. Nothing. And when I look back at her struggles, I'm happy that she had them years with James. They were so close and content - at least she had that."

There had been a quality of unreality about James' death and Mary Kate remembered the change in her grandmother, the haggardness in her face, the constant sighs - she had not realized at the time the vastness of her sorrow.

She looked at her mother gratefully before she said, "Thank you for this afternoon - for explaining. I feel closer to you today than … than I've ever done. I'm no longer smarting."

"Thanks for that Mary Kate. I'm sixty-seven years old and I'll always be glad that I lived to see this day and to spend this precious time with you."

"You look well preserved for your years."

She smiled softly, "Thanks. Andrew's been good to me and I have him to thank for my good fortune." Mary Kate reached across the table and pressed her mother's hand, grateful because she had revealed so much of the hidden past, so much of her inner self. She began buttering the pile of bread again, "We better get these sandwiches made."

Secrets on the Breeze

The two women worked in silence, each reflecting on what had gone on before.

Leaning heavily on her stick, Sara made her way slowly into the sitting room.

She stood for a moment looking around the familiar room. She nodded in satisfaction at the re-upholstered furnishing, the deep red velvet curtains and the matching rugs. Glancing around the walls, she looked again at James' paintings and sighed softly in memory. She remembered the day they laid him to rest. A light wind blew damply across the sea, an eerie half-light wreathed Clougher churchyard as James' body was consigned at last in the Donegal earth he had loved so much.

Mary Kate watched her, unseen from the hallway.

She was very still. She had her back to the light and suddenly she had a glimpse of the woman she had been fifty years ago, hypnotic in her stillness, graceful in her movements, capable of just about any task and an overwhelming compassion for everyone who came into her circle.

When she moved slowly to her armchair and was seated, Mary Kate went in, signalling for the fiddle player to follow. Soon the room was filled with people.

They greeted her in turn to the strains of 'happy birthday'. Her surprise and delight at seeing Maura, Andrew and her grandsons, brought tears to Mary Kate's eyes.

Sara received a steady stream of visitors and towards evening Sally came and proudly introduced her husband-to-be to Sara, "My mother," she told him, "life only began for me when I came to this house." When the celebration was finally over, Mary Kate and Maura helped the old woman into bed. Although tired and feeble, a youthful vigour shone in her eyes, "Thank you for a grand day. All of you, each and every one, have made an old woman happy." Then looking at Mary Kate she said, "I've been thinking about poor Eleanor a lot lately. I wish she could have had a family like I have. It would have made up for all the pain of her youth - all them secrets she had to keep," she said sleep beginning to close her eyelids.

Mary Kate sat alone by the smouldering turf fire, until she saw the headlights of his car coming up the driveway. She had opened the big hall door before he reached it. "So good to be home," Colin said, kissing her softly on the lips.

They walked along the driveway hand in hand for a little way and stood listening to the whispers of the night, before turning back towards the house. They went inside and he closed the door behind him. They were alone. The hall was eerily quiet as if all the ghosts of the old house had gathered to listen to their conversation.

"I have some news for you," he said softly, "We are

going to be grandparents. I saw James yesterday evening and he gave me the news that he and Mary are expecting a new arrival next January. I wish I could tell her right away," he said, nodding towards the stairs.

"It'll keep till the morning," she said as they climbed the stairs together.

Hazel McIntyre